# A Near-Perfect Gift

R. M. KINDER

THE UNIVERSITY OF MICHIGAN PRESS
*Ann Arbor*

2008   2007   2006   2005     4   3   2   1

*A CIP catalog record for this book is available from the British Library.*

Library of Congress Cataloging-in-Publication Data

Kinder, R. M. (Rose Marie)
    A near-perfect gift / R. M. Kinder.
        v.      cm.
    Contents: Going into battle — Ghosts — Madman's moon — Pulse of
the world — The promise — A winter snake — Searching for heroes —
Blue baby — A near-perfect gift — An intimate gesture — Friday
fishermen — Late fall — With a change of seasons.
    ISBN 0-472-03106-6 (pbk. : alk. paper)
    I. Title.
    PS3561.I429N43    2005
    813'.54—dc22                                        2005003518

*To*
⊰ *Kristine Allana Lowe–Martin,* ⊱
*my sharpest critic and editor,*
*kindest reader, and dearest ally*

# ⊰Acknowledgments⊱

"An Intimate Gesture," *Short Story* 5, no. 1 (1997): 8–20

"Ghosts," *Connecticut Review* 22, no. 1 (2000): 99–101

"Going into Battle," *Jabberwock* 21, no. 1 (1999): 7–23

"Late Fall," *Icon* (Spring 1994): 6–10

"Madman's Moon," *Ogalala Review* 6 (1996): 29–35

"A Near-Perfect Gift," *Southern Humanities Review* 33, no. 1 (Winter 1999): 64–77

"Pulse of the World," *Writer's Digest 1996 Winners' Booklet*

"Searching for Heroes," *Southern Indiana Review* 10, no. 1 (2003): 67–82

"A Winter Snake," *Appalachian Heritage* 22, no. 4 (1994): 57–63

"With a Change of Seasons," *CutBank* 15 (1980): 63–76

# Contents

# ⊰ Going into Battle ⊱

Onie and Old Lady Buckroe didn't quite live in Box Town, but at its edge. Their houses were on the upper rim, near the junction where the asphalt road dipped deeply, forming a steep V into which the factory had once dumped all its refuse, including the gigantic cardboard boxes that gave the area its name. Down the V and up the other side were crumbling houses, among them the homes of two of my buddies, Johnny Matson and Paul Welford. From the first grade on, Richard Tilley and I would wait at the top of the hill for the others to join us and we'd walk the upper road together. Sometimes we catcalled to Onie's or Buckroe's house or chanted some song about fat ladies, crazy ladies. By the time we were ending fifth grade, we had decided that the two women were witches. The belief especially took our fancy late that summer and grew more intense when school began. Perhaps it seemed plausible because none of us actually believed in witches at all, and so it was safe to act as if we did.

Onie was between fifty and eighty, and was, as most kids in town knew, a welfare case. We boys assumed that marked her as inferior, fair game for taunting. Some people claimed Onie's brother actually supported her, and quite well—she just didn't do anything with the money. Her yard was mostly dirt, shaded by immense walnut trees, and she never picked up the walnuts. They lay green, then brown, black, year after year, only a few of them disappearing with the squirrels. Onie herself was an obese, brownish woman, either from naturally darkish skin or from never bathing. She was filthy about her person and her living conditions. She wore shapeless dresses, often with the sleeves torn out to accommodate the swell of her enormous arms. Sometimes, if the weather were cool, she wore two or three dresses at once. My mother said Onie had dropsy, her legs suppurated, and that accounted for the bandages she often wore around her heavy calves. Probably the bandages caused the most frightening and disgusting aspect of Onie: an unbearable stench if one came too near. On holidays, even just May Day, I had to go with my sisters to deliver a plate of food to Onie. I always tried to stand behind the girls, believing that only women should have to visit women—men had their own burdens. Once, as either punishment or education, my mother made me go alone. "You find something nice to say," she added. "Silence is hard to bear at times. Sometimes it's an insult." That day Onie offered me a glass of water, and I genuinely believed I'd die if I drank it. It had the light rust color of all our tap water, but I feared it was dirt— from Onie. I held the glass till I came up with "I hope you're feeling good." Then, dizzy from nausea, I placed the glass next to her chair and bolted out the door.

"So, she gave you water," my mother said later, during her standard interrogation about duty assigned and duty fulfilled. "And did you stay till you drank it?"

"I put the glass right next to her when I left."

"Full or empty?"

"Right between."

I got away, though we both knew I'd insulted Onie. Guests were to drink what they were given. Period.

My friend Johnny had another belief about Onie's smell. It wasn't dropsy, he said. "It's putrid rot. She sold her soul to the devil and can't die. You wait. She'll rot all over and still be walking around."

Johnny had something wrong with himself, too. He was skinny and dark, and his arms and legs were often scaly, sometimes even scabbed. My mother thought it might be impetigo and said I should avoid skin contact if possible. She let me play with him, though, and I didn't worry about his skin. Neither did Richard or Paul. Years later, when Johnny joined the Marines, his skin was smooth, stretched tight over well-earned, wiry muscles.

The other witch was Letitia Buckroe, Old Lady Buckroe. She was somewhere between sixty and eighty, and about the same size as Onie, only very pale, talcum-powder pale, and scrupulously clean. Paul's sister had to go to Old Lady Buckroe's every Sunday and help lace her corset. Paul described it as he had heard it, how the powder billowed up and out with each tug, suffocating the lacer. It gave his sister asthma attacks, Paul said, but she couldn't get out of going, because "there's no one else to do it for her."

"You could do it for her, Paul," Johnny said, and we all laughed. Johnny mimicked garroting the old woman with her corset lace, and we laughed at that, too. When he mimicked holding up massive breasts, we were down to just smiling and looking at one another. We were young enough for possible violence to be humorous, but old enough for possible sex to be threatening.

We knew Old Lady Buckroe had to be a witch because of her husband's condition. We decided maybe she had done something to him. He was a pale sliver of a man, so thin we could see the shape of his fine bones under his skin, but very handsome. He roamed Mrs. Buckroe's yard as though he were tethered there by an invisible line. At the edge of the sidewalk or the mown grass, he'd stop and stare vacantly like only a void lay beyond, or an ocean maybe, some kind of expanse he couldn't brave alone. Sometimes he entered the long shed at the back end of Mrs. Buckroe's lot, and stayed there till she called to him. "Eddie," she'd say two or three times, and eventually he'd shuffle toward her, though he rarely looked up. She always dressed him in clothes ironed creased and stiff. Part of his forehead was gone, as if a sculptor had missed that one curve. The tissue there was smooth in the center, but jagged at the edges, and met the rest of the skin like a layer of lace woven in. When I sat near Mr. Buckroe in church on Sunday, I couldn't not look at that scar. My fingertips yearned to touch it.

Paul felt that way, too. "It's like magic," he said, and shuddered.

"No, it's witchcraft," Johnny said. "Maybe he didn't obey her. Maybe he caught onto her and was going to turn her in."

"Maybe he was going to burn her," I said. "That's what you have to do with witches. That, or mash them with stones, or drown them."

4

The others got quiet then. We were in the bottom of the dry ditch behind my house, and we could hear the slight breeze whooshing in the trees above. It was mid-September, and we could still go out after supper. Soon, we'd be kept in every night, watching frost form on the windows outside, watching television shows our folks would allow, and being lily white until spring. We were fairly somber, and a subject like witches suited our mood.

"Only if they're black witches," I added. I had done my encyclopedia assignment on witches and felt on sure ground, but I wanted to be fair about it all.

"What's the difference?"

"White ones just do good stuff. They're more into herbs and candles and things like that."

"A witch is a witch is a witch," Johnny said. "And we got two of them on our hands."

"We can't do anything, anyhow," Paul said. "If we have to drown them or . . ."

"Press or burn."

"Or press or burn. We can't do something like that."

"We can exorcise them, maybe."

Everyone looked at me with that. We had all seen the *Exorcist*. Richard's brother had taped the movie and let us see it for a dollar apiece. I could still see that girl's head turn all around on her body—that and other things. I kept my older sister's silver cross under my pillow at night, to ward off evil I might not be able to handle. Her boyfriend had given it to her. She gave up on finding where she'd lost it and bought another one to wear to church. Then they only cost three dollars or so, but she got more allowance than I did.

5

"Can you exorcise a witch?" from Paul.

"I don't see why not," Johnny said. "You can exorcise a devil, and they got to be harder."

"How do you do it?"

I didn't know and neither did anyone else, but we decided on a way then and there. We knew we had to get something personal, pieces of hair, fingernails, clothing. And we needed protection, my cross, certainly, but a Bible, too.

"And a flashlight." Paul's eyes were already sort of wild. "Witches like the dark," he said. "We can spook them off with a flashlight." Paul was afraid of the dark. We all knew that.

"And the Bible?" Johnny looked at me. I pointed to Richard. His mother kept a big one on their coffee table. It was gold, with a painted picture of Jesus on the cover.

"No," Richard said. "Mom'd beat me to death." That wasn't true, and we knew it. If anyone ever said anything unkind to Richard, his face would blush so red it'd hurt the sayer. He was jolly and happy, and fat. He was never willing to do anything, either, unless he was coerced. But he couldn't take pressure. After we all stared at him for awhile, he muttered, "Okay, okay, okay." And thus we had our ammo for our own kind of war.

Johnny leaned back on his heels. "Well, my friends," he said, "we are on a witchhunt."

It was a somber moment. The shadows of the trees lining the ditch fell across us, and though they had probably been there all along, we noticed them at that moment, together. Maybe a cloud had just passed over the sun.

"Look." Paul nodded at the flat limestone we had circled around.

"What is it?" from Richard.

"That shadow's a cross," Paul said in his little whisper voice.

"Jesus," Johnny said.

Richard stood up quickly. "That's profanity," he said. "I don't know anything about witches, but I know profanity when I hear it. And saying 'Jesus' like that is profanity. I'm going home."

"Tomorrow afternoon," Johnny called, standing willowy and brown. "Here. Three thirty."

We did meet the next day, but it didn't do much good because one or the other of us kept foreseeing problems. We'd have to get in Onie's place in the daytime, while she was sitting on the front porch, but she might hear us. Her back steps creaked like crazy, and the back door might be locked. Old Lady Buckroe was inside most of the time, so we could at least get in her shed, just by pulling out one of the rotten boards. But it would have to be on Sunday, when she was in church, or after dark, when she couldn't see us. For both witches, we needed a diversion.

Richard and Paul, of course, wanted to be the diversion.

"How do you know she's in the house after dark?" Paul asked. "Maybe she's in the shed working her magic."

"Witchcraft. Magic's something else."

"What else?"

I knew, but I wasn't sure how to explain it then. One

was okay and one wasn't. One hurt people and the other pleased them.

"They could both be in that shed," Paul continued. "They could be there waiting on us." He looked at me. "They can tell the future, can't they?"

I said I thought so.

We had to meet over the weekend, too. Richard had his mother's Bible on Sunday afternoon, and he had his own Sunday-school testament in his shirt pocket. "I'm going to carry this little one every day," he said, "no matter what you guys think. It's my personal protection."

We put the big gold Bible on the limestone. Johnny put his hand on the center of it and closed his eyes a minute. That seemed right enough that the rest of us did it in turns. I was hoping the shadow cross would appear again, just at that moment, but it didn't. Still, it felt safe, the four of us laying hands on the Bible together. Later, when we were climbing out of the ditch, I looked back, and there again was the shadow on the limestone. I liked that, the mystery of timing and everything. At that age nothing is coincidence. And every sign is for your personal happiness.

On Monday, as soon as we had each reported home— Johnny had to call his mother at work and I had to show my face to my sister, who "babysat" me—we met at the south end of the witches' street. I told the guys we couldn't come in from the north, because that's a witch's direction and we needed all the opposite power we could get. Paul and Richard were to push Paul's bicycle, coming up from the south, but on the east side of the street. They were supposed to stop opposite Onie's house, and then cross over. One of them was to ask her for a bicycle pump, which she sure wasn't going to have. Then they'd act like they just saw the green walnut shells and needed a few, for ringworm. If she said no, they'd hang around and keep grabbing walnuts. She'd get mad and stumble up from her old rocker and try to get off the porch, and they'd stay a few yards ahead of her.

"She's on the porch now," Johnny said. "You guys keep her there."

They nodded.

"You'll do it for sure, right? We can count on you?"

They nodded again, two timid eleven-year-olds before their master.

They didn't do anything we had planned, neither the bicycle pump nor the walnut ruse, but of course Johnny and I didn't know that. We cut across the Wilsons' yard, by the old ruins of the Nazarene church—just four partial walls, some blackened with the fire that had burned it down before I was born—and sneaked bent over and fast up Onie's yard to beneath her back stairs. They stretched loose and long, like a sideways ladder. We scrunched among honeysuckle vines and milkweed and a pile of old magazines all mildewed into one.

"Who's going up, you or me?" Johnny had his firm look on, his mouth twisting with his words, his dark eyes meeting mine like we were going into battle.

"Together," I said.

We crept out and up. Johnny had one hand against the house, and I held onto the railing. At the door, we paused. He pulled out the screen door very gently, and I held it open while he pressed his ear against the glass of the inside door. He turned the knob slowly and pushed.

9

It opened. With a deep breath and a brave look at me, he moved inward. So did I.

The house stank. It was the sickest smell. Dense, maybe like bad perfume, or old fruit. I was queasy. I vomit easily, anyhow. Inherited my father's stomach, my mother said.

Nothing in that kitchen had ever been clean. Nothing had ever been put away. Pans were stacked on the stove and on the counter. Plants were everywhere, long vines falling onto browned newspapers on the kitchen table, hanging from the refrigerator, from wire hooks in the ceiling.

"Hair and fingernails," Johnny said, and I nodded.

We moved on. The hallway was very short, and halfway down Johnny mouthed "bathroom" and stepped from the hall. I looked into the living room and saw Onie's shape through the window to the porch.

"She's still on the porch," I whispered. "She's right outside."

"Get in here," I heard.

I stepped inside the bathroom with him and almost gagged.

"This ought to do," he said.

He was holding one of Onie's leg bandages up above the trash can. Looking at it sickened me. I didn't know how he could touch it.

In the hallway again, he turned toward her bedroom.

"Where you going?" I said. "We got enough."

"Just looking."

Her bedroom was piled up, too. I could see Johnny's reflection in the mirror, all spidery from the old glass. He was rummaging among tissues and clothing on the dresser. He lifted something—I saw it glint—and hurried around the foot of the bed.

"Got it," he said. "Let's get out of here."

She was still rocking on the front porch when we cleared the hallway. We had left the kitchen door open, and the sweet smell of outside drew me. I thought about leaving the door open again, but didn't. She could bring in her own fresh air.

We were down the steps when we saw Mr. Buckroe watching us. His head was lifted, and he stood as rigid as a weather vane. One of his arms came partway up, stiff, like a puppet arm.

"He knows," I stammered, "so she does, too."

"Run." We both dashed south, by the burnt walls, across the Wilsons' yard, to the street.

Paul and Richard were there, standing on the culvert.

"Some diversion," I said. "If this had been war, we'd be dead and you two would get dishonorable discharges."

They just shrugged and dug their hands in their pockets. Richard was red. Paul was studying what Johnny had stolen, what we had stolen, I suppose.

Johnny held up the bandage and a glass bowl. "Mission accomplished."

"My mom has one of those," Paul said. "It's a hairsaver. Women save their hair and stuff pillows with it."

"Sick." But that wasn't exactly how I felt.

Paul and Richard said they couldn't do a diversion because Old Lady Buckroe and her husband had been in the front yard.

"They teamed up on us," Paul said. "She was in the north and she had him pointed right at us."

We certainly understood their fear. If she could maneuver her skeleton man around, no telling what she could do to us. If she caught us.

We carried our loot to the ditch.

"I think it's gotta be one ceremony for both witches," Johnny said. "Or should we do Onie now? Exorcise her alone? Will that make them weaker?"

They all looked at me. "One ceremony," I said. "If you want to knock somebody down, you get both legs, right?"

Johnny liked my answer. "We gotta get Buckroe soon, then," he said. "We can't let them talk it over. Maybe we should go tonight."

"Not tonight." I wasn't feeling too well. "Paul and Richard probably wouldn't be up to it."

We decided we couldn't wait until Sunday morning, though, because Old Lady Buckroe might not go to church and we might not be able to avoid going. We had to do it the next night. I told them how they had to think white, to keep only good thoughts all the time, just like we had to do when we took the Lord's Supper on Sundays at my church. And this time, we had to go in together, the four of us.

"One for each corner of the earth," I told them, "and armed with the words and sign of God."

"I can't get the big Bible except on Sunday," Richard said.

"Sure you can," from Johnny. "Tell them my mother wants to use the concordance."

"That's a lie."

"But it's to kill a witch," Paul said, and that settled the

matter except that he added, "I mean to exorcise a witch. To exorcise two witches."

"We know what you meant," I said.

Johnny tried to get me to keep the bandage and bowl, but I wouldn't touch them. He wrapped them in a newspaper I'd brought from the house. I guess he put them in his closet or dresser at home. I wouldn't have been able to sleep. Things rub off or get in the air. Fear is contagious.

The next night Johnny called each of our parents and asked if we could come over. His mother was on the swing shift, and sometime he got nervous by himself.

"You're welcome to stay here," my dad offered, but Johnny said he was supposed to stay home and he wanted to obey his mother. My dad drove me over there instead, and Paul's mother drove up at the same time. She had Richard with her, too.

"I don't like the looks of this," she said. My dad talked to her for a few minutes, where we couldn't hear, then called that he'd be back at nine o'clock sharp. Together they had decided to trust us.

It was about six thirty then. We waited until seven. When we got to the south street junction, we could see both houses okay. The living room light was on at Onie's place. We couldn't tell about Buckroe's because of the streetlight in front. It made everything pale silver and clear, but ugly clear. The flower beds didn't look real, and the flowers weren't orange and yellow, just clumps of white glare.

We stopped first inside the Nazarene walls, because that seemed like the best spot. Each of us had a flashlight. Paul had a testament like Richard's. Richard had his mother's gold Bible. I had my silver cross. "You need something," I told Johnny, and he pulled out this tiny blue bottle.

"That's perfume," Paul said. "My mom's got some. It's French."

" 'Evening in Paris,' " Johnny said, seeming older with such specific, and strange, knowledge. "But if we bless it," Johnny said, "it's holy water."

We put the bottle on the gold Bible and laid the cross and testaments next to it. Then Paul recited the Lord's Prayer. He had a real good memory. We all said Amen.

Richard lugged the big Bible with him, despite our insistence that he wouldn't be much help so weighted down. He held it with both hands, like a tray, and had his flashlight right in the center of it. He had to walk carefully to keep it from rolling off.

"You're the Gateman," I said.

"What's that?"

"Like the lookout." I'd seen a number of movies when my sister watched them. All I had to do was sit just outside my bedroom door and lean forward. She knew, but then she knew I could hear her and her boyfriend when they were on the front porch. We had a good relationship.

The streetlight didn't reach behind the shed. There, in the alley, we knelt on the sloping dirt and tried to pull loose one of the shed boards. Johnny got a splinter in his hand, and Richard, armed with his precious flashlight, pulled it out. I was just slipping my fingers under the same board when Paul whispered me out of the way. He had a limb, thin at one end and thick at the other. He squatted down and pushed it in and up until two wooden slats splintered. Then he grasped the raw edges and cracked them back and off. "That's my part," he said. Johnny and I together broke off enough rotten sections that we could crawl in easily. Paul came only halfway, and stayed on his hands and knees. Richard, I guess, stood out there quivering with his guiding light.

It was dark inside. I could hear Johnny breathing and was thankful for the sound and frightened at the intensity that made me hear it. The air smelled like wet dirt, maybe like an old cellar, where water has stood for too long. Odd shapes, all one-dimensional shadows, loomed around us, and, if I moved my eyes too quickly, seemed to lunge just as I looked away. "Come on," Johnny whispered. "Let's get some of her stuff. Something we can burn."

"Not me," hissed from the opening, and Paul was, I knew, gone.

The shadows began to take form. Shelves, tables, boxes of books, planters. A lawn mower stood by one side of the door. Chairs were stacked on the other side. A porch swing was on the dirt floor, and I remembered that Old Lady Buckroe used to sit in a swing on her front porch. Johnny, bent over a little and moving toward one end of the shed, suddenly fell. He gasped and scrambled sideways and up, flashing his light down. It was a garden hose, all coiled and tied still.

My heart wouldn't believe it was a garden hose. Witch hands were everywhere. "Let's go," I said. "We're not going to find anything."

"Wanna bet?"

He was standing near an old trunk. He lifted the lid,

and I looked inside with him. The top was a divided tray, cardboard, the paper curling brown, and filled with packets of letters tied in twine. We leafed through two packets. "Pvt. Edward Buckroe" said each return address, "Mrs. Edward Buckroe" the one being written to. My dad had been in the service. Johnny thought his had been, too. He couldn't be sure. Beneath the tray were folded uniforms. "Army," Johnny said, fingering dark cloth.

"Shut it, okay? We shouldn't be going through his stuff."

"In a minute." He slipped the twine from one packet, and lifted the flap of one of the letters.

"Don't read it," I said.

"Maybe it tells what happened to him."

I couldn't read it from where I stood, but I could see the print he had used, strong and firm, quick. Hurried, I guess. He had been in a real war.

"Put it back," I said.

Johnny folded the pages along the same creases. For a minute I thought he was going to put it in his pocket, but then he returned it to the envelope and the packet.

Maybe Old Lady Buckroe had seen our flashlights or heard the cracking of wood at the back of her shed. Maybe Pvt. Edward Buckroe had. Maybe he staked the place out at night. At any rate, something was rattling the shed door, and I was up, intending to backside out of there, but I didn't get the chance. Light suddenly sprang all around us, and I was momentarily breathless and frozen still. Old Lady Buckroe stood in the open doorway, hand on a wall switch. Who knew the shed had electricity? Many homes in that area of town didn't have inside bathrooms. Mrs. Buckroe seemed unusually big, draped in some kind of purple robe, white hair down and around her shoulders. Johnny bolted for the hole we'd made, and I ran around the trunk, behind a long table covered with tools, and just dashed right past her. She said my name. I remember I was surprised that she knew it. Knew it all, I mean, even the middle one. I ran right into him, Mr. Buckroe, Pvt. Edward Buckroe. He stumbled backward and fell, and I landed right beside him, close enough to look directly in his eyes. They were blue, but it was as if the blue had started to run into the white and the white was turning yellow. And they bulged, like they were going to pop out at me. I was up and running again. Nothing like that was ever going to touch me, not if I could run. Behind me, she was saying his name now. "Eddie. Eddie." I noticed then, and remember now, that voices don't sound old.

I was halfway home before I remembered that my father was going to pick me up at Johnny's. I ran back that way, skirting by yards to avoid the upper road. There were no streetlights in his part of town, no porch lights, and I clutched the cross as I ran by hedges no one trimmed, and trees no one pruned, and across a gravel, rutted driveway to Johnny's house. When I stepped on the porch, he came around the side of the house and joined me.

Richard and Paul never showed.

"They're long gone," Johnny said. "They were probably gone the minute we got inside."

It was very dark on his porch, and quiet. The whole place was musty, damp. I hadn't realized how lonely Box Town could be at night. At least we were together, two kids with the adult world probably mad at them and ganging up against them. Johnny, though, was usually down here alone. I was understanding what that meant.

"What'd it say?" I asked. "The letter?"

He was running his fingers along the rough edge of the porch. Against that white, his skin looked almost burned. "Nothing," he said.

"Sure it did. You read it. I saw you."

"It was hard to read. I didn't get much."

"You're not any older than I am. And I helped you get in there."

He considered this, tearing a blade of grass into tiny pieces. "Some of it was love stuff. He talked about a friend of his getting killed. Blown to pieces. Stuff like that."

The moon hung orange straight above the V. We were in the very bottom of Box Town, where nothing was ever really good, or new, or even lasted long. It was a place to leave, and that was scary when you didn't know any other places.

"Did he say he was afraid?" I wasn't sure I wanted to know the answer, but the question had to be asked.

"Nope." Johnny held a grass blade up to his lips as if it were a cigarette, then tried to flick it away. "Not him. Not Private Edward Buckroe."

I think maybe Johnny lied to me. If so, I certainly understand. I would have done the same for him.

"Think she'll tell on us?" I asked.

"Sure. We're gonna pay," he said.

Obviously that was okay by him.

When a car came down the hill, slowly, precisely on the right side, I knew it was my father, whether or not it was nine o'clock.

We all four had to take Onie's bowl back to her. My mother talked with her. She and Johnny's mother went over the next Sunday and did dishes and things like that. Johnny and the rest of us had to clean up under the back stairs and then rake the entire yard. Onie sat on the porch watching us, and it gave me the willies. Our hands turned brown from the walnuts, and the stain wouldn't wash off. I complained to my mother about that, and she made me wear gloves to bed so her sheets would stay clean.

Every Sunday afternoon when the weather was clear enough, I had to walk Old Man Buckroe. I knocked on their door, and Mrs. Buckroe had me come in. It was very hot in there and smelled too sweet. I knew it was her powder. Sometimes traces of it remained on her throat. She bundled her Eddie up in an old black coat and wrapped a red scarf around his neck. She put a hat on his head and gloves on his hands. She stood in the doorway when we headed up the street. I thought Johnny and the others should have had to do it, too, but my dad and mom said Johnny and the others weren't their kids, I was. Mr. Buckroe never said anything. No magic sprang up between us so that I understood what he had felt or longed for or lost. When I walked, he walked. When I stopped, he stopped. He was a spooky old gent. If I met his eyes, he'd stare back watery and gone and not turn away until I did.

I thought about asking Mrs. Buckroe how he got the scar, but I preferred not knowing. Hand grenade or cancer, the effect was the same.

He and I only walked together for a few months. Mrs. Buckroe gathered him back to herself with some gracefully vague mention of "losing control." Eventually, he no longer appeared in the yard. My mother said he was bedridden.

He died while we boys were in high school, and was buried in the Veterans' Cemetery. We didn't go to the funeral. Once, driving by the two houses on a sultry Sunday afternoon, I entertained the idea of asking Onie for a glass of water, and downing the contents before her very eyes. But I didn't do it then, either. The gesture might have been good for me, but I doubt she needed it. She and her neighbor were remarkably strong ladies. They held down the home ground. Lady Buckroe lived into her nineties, with other young girls taking over the lacing of that prodigious corset. Onie became an even crustier old dame, yelling at generations of school kids who marveled at the mystery she presented. Summer days found these ladies much the same, one rocking brown on a creaking, shaded porch, the other all bustling and powdery, saving things for years.

# ⸼ Ghosts ⸼

A ghost lived in Cora's home. His name was Francis and he harmed no one, but made creaking steps through the house, often coming into Cora's room where he stood invisible and silent at the foot of her bed, so that if she moved, if she took even one breath, he might, just might, become violent and choke her or stab her to death, in her very home, and wouldn't that be terrible? Awful? It gave them both shivers. Katy's house held a skeleton, a man killed probably hundreds of years ago, who bided his time in the attic, waiting for someone who didn't know better to open the attic door just once, just the slightest not-even-inch, and his soul would seep through that bare crack and get revenge on the first warm flesh he found, which would likely be Katy or Cora since Katy's bed was directly beneath the attic square.

When the summer nights were clear and the sun lately setting, one of the two little girls would run, pajamas clutched in slender arms or wadded into a paper sack, along the uneven sidewalks between their houses, and come into the other's home all flushed with stories of possible dangers just passed, a shadow behind a bush, a sudden noise, a stranger on a porch, a dark house. They would talk with the at-home parent awhile, answering questions about school or family, and sneak looks and quick smiles at one another, with much hiding behind small, curved hands or with dropped eyes. Then came bedtime, and they would sit in the middle of the bed, whispering. They dared not fall asleep, they dared not.

But of course they did, wrapped around each other, one dark haired and rosy skinned, the other blond and golden.

In each home, a wraith-man came and went, after hours, when all was dark and ghosts and skeletons and suchlike were held at bay by little-girl dreams. At Cora's, the man staggered down the hall, mumbling magic curses, into her mother's bedroom and was transformed overnight to a gentle morning mute. At Katy's, the man crept silently, into and out of her mother's bed before dawn, and left only gaps of chill in the air and brown clouds in her mother's eyes. The girls never spoke of these nighttime creatures, though sometimes they heard them and waited their passing together.

They grew older, Katy turning round, with an uplifted nose and wild blond curls, Cora becoming more slender, freckles forever permanent, hair teasing red. But still they liked one another, nodding in the school halls, waving from groups of other friends. Once they encountered each other midday, the bell having rung, and they at false liberty. In a moment, they were gone, out of the building, chattering to Katy's home while fall leaves spiraled in the streets. They dressed in her mother's half-slips as evening gowns, pulled up over young breasts, falling to young shins, and they giggled over pickle juice served as wine in green dessert dishes.

Another time they came together at the corner store, and sat one brief hour under the bridge spanning the drainage ditch, where Katy smoked many cigarettes and Cora vomited after two. Katy had many boyfriends then, and Cora had none. Katy said "Look" and touched her own nipples, and they sprang out like hard, wonderful buttons. Then she leaned to rub Cora's nipples through the soft sweater. "See," Katy said. "That's what they do just looking at me."

Katy came down stairs so her breasts bounced. In classes, she crossed her legs with their dimpled knees and swung her foot backward and forward, backward and forward, the gold chain with the boy's name draped right at her ankle. Cora stuffed tissue in her bra and daubed lemon juice on freckles in the midnight moonlight, and stood with groups of girls next to groups of boys. Still, they sometimes looked at one another, just for a moment, with a half-smile or a half-turn, almost a spoken word.

"She's not so bad," Katy said. "You guys don't know what she's like. And yeah, she used to be a friend of mine. A good friend."

"Katy wouldn't do that," Cora said. "She likes boys, but she's not as rough as you think. I've known her a long time. We used to play together."

Cora moved away, and Katy stayed. Each married. Moons rose and faded. Years came and went. Katy lay in bed at night, gold still but wire thin, eyes wide and dark from factory days and little money and children not blessed with health. She heard of Cora, all fair and fine, gone some thousand miles away. Cora dreamed of small towns and forever first loves and children running in real grass over unfenced yards and husbands whose hands still touched their wives.

"I have got to get out of here," each said to dark nights alone.

Then for one brief span Cora sat on her mother's porch, the evening moist and humming with fireflies and crickets, while Katy walked the uneven sidewalk for a moment's peace, and there they were. Neither said, "You look the same." Neither cried. They kissed. They sat on the step side by side, holding hands. They talked of skeletons and ghosts and of not being able to move for centuries.

# ⊰ Madman's Moon ⊱

Travis Kratz may have wanted to say a number of things, but the only words we ever heard him speak were "You got a quarter?" and "Want me do a jig?"

He was a moron, a genuine one, a clinical one, and he was ugly, even if innocence should have made him cute. He had a narrow face, a slack, back-sloping jaw, black wild hair, and bug eyes. His teeth were bucked, too, and wide spaced, and he grinned wet drippy grins all the time.

After he was about thirteen, he roamed the country-side outside Buxton, and the town itself, pretty much at will. He was big then, much bigger than his father, which is probably why he was just let loose on the rest of us. People who didn't lock their doors—and there were many of them in our area—would come home to find dishes in their sinks or crumbs on their table, and know that Travis had been there. Sometimes quarters would be missing from change bowls or tops of dressers, or at least people thought some quarters were gone. Travis liked shiny things very much, but he didn't want dimes or nickels, even half-dollars. He'd hand those back, no matter how many someone gave him, and look morose until a quarter was offered. He'd snatch that.

He also liked music, though he had no more rhythm than a sun-fried toad. He'd come into the bus station where we all hung out on weekends, and play the juke-box, picking songs at random, with no concept of a quarter's worth. He'd just continue punching buttons until the music started. Then he'd begin his own dance, jerking all over and tossing slobbery looks to make sure we saw him. When his quarters were gone, or when the manager of the station ran him off, he'd hustle people, stop them on the street, block their path, say, "Want me do a jig? You got a quarter?" He'd sidestep, walk backward, and if they kept going, just look puzzled, like, what did he do wrong?

None of us really minded Travis until he did get so big, and so free. He started appearing on Saturday nights, when we'd dance in the back room of the bus station. The room had been added on just to give teenage Buxton a place to go where parents could drop in or telephone. Travis would lean against the raw-wood wall, one foot braced behind him like he'd seen us do. His jeans were too tight, his arms and legs too firm for him to be really an idiot. If it weren't for his expression, a dumb-dog hunger, he could have been just one of the guys.

Then he began watching the girls. If one would look at him, he'd go into his jig routine, and it wasn't funny. It shamed us, at least the guys. We wanted him out of there, and got the manager to call Travis's parents to keep him away at nighttime. He still showed up, though, and we figured maybe, just maybe, he pushed his mother and father out of the way. He was certainly strong enough to do it. But that was a little hard to believe, since Travis to our knowledge had never used force on anything. He even brushed his bristly hair back gently, as if he could baby-pat it in place. The gesture was his version of the slick hair-stroke of some of the guys.

One Saturday, though, Becky Weaver said she had seen Travis in her yard the night before, standing right near the fence that separated yard from barnyard.

"I was putting on my pajamas," she said, her eyes all dark and guarded. "I was in front of my window because, after all, we live in the country and I'm on the second floor. I got this feeling like something was watching me, and there he was in my backyard."

"Was he looking at you?"

"He had been." She shivered. "I knew that right away."

"It was the vapor light," someone said. "Travis likes lights."

We all knew that was probably right. I'd seen him kind of hypnotized by the new traffic light south of the courthouse. He had stood on the corner while it changed colors five times—I counted the changes. Eventually he moved on. Travis had too much energy to stay put for long. He was bursting with energy, and good health. If he hadn't been an idiot, he probably could have bested any of us.

Becky insisted, though, that he had been looking at her. She said girls could tell about things like that.

"He knew I saw him, and he took off. It scares me a little," she said. "What if my folks had been gone? What if he had come in the house? Maybe that's what he planned to do."

Someone said that Travis couldn't make plans. "He can barely say a complete sentence. You think he can hold a plan in his head?"

"Well, I'm scared of him," Becky said. "He looks at me all the time."

"Did you tell your dad?"

"No. I wouldn't want him to shoot Travis or anything."

One of my mother's favorite words about young people was "coy." She used it lots of ways. "Don't be coy, now," she'd say to me. "You know what I'm talking about." Often I did. Becky was the prettiest of the girls in our group, and usually guys were looking at her, even if they pretended they weren't. But sometimes Becky made too much of herself, and we all knew that, too.

Maybe we didn't believe Becky was really scared, but the idea sort of took hold. We decided it might be wise to follow Travis a few nights, and find out exactly what he did. If he was peeking in girls' windows, something had to be done. There was a house for people like him in Sikeston, and an institution in Fielder, and if he was dangerous, we thought we should know before he did anything, instead of afterward, which is the modern way.

At first it was fun, tracing his loping walk along Buxton's empty streets. It's a hilly town, and we could creep without headlights up and down side streets and intersect Travis's path whenever we wanted. Often we'd park a block or so ahead and watch through the back window of the car. Travis saw us, of course, but we knew we didn't actually register in that dim mind. On he'd trot. If he left the sidewalk, one of us would slip out and cut through a backyard or two, running bent over and slipping on the night grass, till he spied Travis. It didn't take us long to figure out that we had been right all along—he was drawn to yard lights. He seemed determined to find every pole light in Buxton, as if he were mapping the town.

"It was just the vapor light," one of us said. "Becky isn't going to like that at all."

We could have let it go then, could have let old Travis stalk his little pleasures. But there wasn't much to do in a town our size, and other than the bus station on weekend nights, excitement was hard to come by. We had no movie theater. It had closed years before, after an old man had been arrested. He would stand outside and buy some little girl a ticket and a box of Boston Baked Beans. Then, during the show, he'd slide his hand along her thigh and up to her panties. The manager spotted him one Saturday afternoon and called the sheriff. They motioned him out of the row. Some little girls from our area testified against him. Helen Walters was one of them. That was in our grade-school years, and we still thought about it when we looked at Helen.

One of us suggested that Travis was like a night-blind deer. We could probably catch him with a flashlight. We all laughed. The idea, though, stayed, like such ideas usually do. We got the biggest flashlights our folks had and kept them in the car with us. We'd drive by Travis walking and flick them toward him a few times, like saying "Come here, boy." We could crisscross him, X him with lights. Then we'd zip away. The light always stopped him dead, but when we drove on, he'd lope after us a few feet.

"He knows it's us."

"Nah. He doesn't even know who he is, much less who we are."

One night two of us got out at what served as the town park, a dark, small field just before the city-limits sign. It was the farthest reach of Travis's south-town run. The park's east side, where the bleachers were, met Buxton's main road. The other three sides sloped up into gradually deepening woods. Buxton had once been swampland, and the park ground itself was always musty, ringing with the sound of frogs and katydids. Four of us ran across the field to the south rim and stationed ourselves behind some blackberry bushes. We pushed the flashlights into the tangles and waited till we got the signal from the guys in the car that Travis was coming. Side by side we turned them on and off, snaking beams across the field. "Here, Travis," one of us whispered. "Here boy, good boy."

We didn't know for a long time if it was working, but then we saw Travis looming at the edge of the park, just to the side of the bleachers. He stood real still. Then he walked a few feet into the field and stopped again. He did this over and over, and it got eerie watching. He inched his way forward, walking sort of sideways like he was stalking us more than we were luring him.

"I don't want him coming over here," someone said, and we tacitly agreed. We turned off the flashlights. But Travis didn't leave. The warm night air hummed with mosquitoes; we had mud on our shoes and finally, from squatting on our heels, mud on the seat of our pants. Two cars had come down the main street, on up to the highway that bypassed town. Still Travis waited. He was a very patient moron.

"It's the moon. He's not paying any attention to us."

He was right. Travis was standing with his face up-ward, mouth agape. Centered in the night sky above was the full summer moon, high and bright, pendent, with nothing holding it there at all.

We left the bushes, just striding onto the field as if we'd been hunting rabbits or squirrels. Travis heard us. He rolled his gaze toward us but was drawn back to the moon. We were at the bleachers when we heard his ragged voice. "You got a quarter?" He was lumbering toward us, that black-bristle hair like a crazy spiked halo. We ran toward the car, got in, and made it home before curfew.

We made the mistake of telling some of the girls about it, and they thought we were "cruel." A couple of them even began saying, "Hi, Travis," when they saw him uptown. We knew they were only getting us back, telling us not to play with the poor fool.

But it was too good to leave alone, like making your own spooky movie.

By the end of summer, before the start of school, we had him dancing beneath the moon. We drew a big cir-cle in the center of the field and told Travis about not crossing lines. "That's a man's rule," we said. We sat outside the circle, and Travis stood in the center. We showed him some dance moves, a little of this one and that one. He could almost copy them. He could drop his eyes to the side and bump his groin forward; he could twist his torso; he could ape-climb his hands while his head bobbed. We enjoyed it all very much. We could get him to do anything we wanted, and that was the most power any of us had ever had. We'd toss a quarter into the ring, and Travis would perform. We taught him to bend from the waist and say over his shoulder, "You got a quarter?" It was funny in the dark. Travis would laugh, too. He would toss his head back and bare his teeth and laugh.

We got the idea to film Travis when we learned one of us had an eight-millimeter camera at home. "My entire babyhood's on film," he said, and talked about his naked parts being saved for posterity. At our urging he spirited it out of the house that Saturday, and we spent a couple of afternoon hours in the bus-station booth, reading the manual. Later, we led Travis through his routine, calling, "Hold it, Travis," "Right there, right there," "Wait a minute, boy, wait a minute." We tried close-ups, too. We had to lie down to angle the camera for a shot of Travis's face with the moon as backdrop, but we got it. That was the week before school began. We didn't get to see the film for two more weeks, and even then it was a quick, hushed affair, because we had only one parentless hour to set up the projector, admire our handiwork, and get back to studying. We agreed we had done pretty well. No one appeared in the film but Travis, and it was a Travis no one in the world knew about but us.

"We could get him to strip," someone said, and we considered that, what we might say, what Travis might do. "Peel it off, boy. There you go." We laughed. We joked about other things we could teach him. But we made no actual plans. We lived in a town where some fathers still strapped the blood out of their children, and where others made their children stand up in church on Sunday morning and make a public apology. We had done about all we could do with Travis, and we knew it.

The old routine was boring, and we couldn't start a more interesting one. So we were finished with Travis the moron, though we drove by the park a few times to see if he was still haunting the grounds. He was. We figured he'd eventually get tired of waiting on us. The weather was cooling, too, and even a fool knows when to come in out of the cold.

We planned a Halloween party at Becky's house, where little kids couldn't be knocking on the door wanting a treat for dressing up. We were way past that kind of fun. We borrowed the projector without permission, each agreeing to take the blame if we got caught, though we weren't certain how to do that. We were going to shock the girls. We knew we were "acting ugly"—my mother's phrase—but we couldn't stop. We weren't hurting anyone. Becky's parents stayed upstairs most of the time, coming to the living room doorway about once every thirty minutes. They let us dance with the lights dim. We danced for a long time, mostly standing still and swaying. When it was getting a little late and Becky's father had just told us we'd have to break up soon, we got the film and projector from the car. We took a chance and turned out all the lights.

We had done very well. There were patches of ground and sky, dizzying swoops from a pair of shoes, up jeaned legs and plaid shirt, to a black sky pinioned by silver dots, but mostly there was just Travis. He was very pale and very happy, intense and ready. His shirt was unbuttoned—we had requested that—and in one frame he pulled the sides back as if baring breasts, strutting and grinning his idiot's grin.

"Shut it off," Helen Walters said.

No one did, and Helen didn't leave the room, though I thought she might. There wasn't a true hero or coward among us. It wasn't that grand then, no battle between good and evil, no Satan under the bed vying for someone's soul. Becky had worn her pink sweater. Another girl had worn a full black skirt, and a fringe of white lace fell from beneath it.

On the screen, Travis bumped forward, and the camera focused on his groin, then his face. He put both hands on his knees and turned his backside to the camera. When he spoke over his shoulder, we couldn't hear his words, but his face showed a request.

"Jesus," Becky whispered. "He scares me to death."

"I bet he does."

The best shot was the last one, when we had framed Travis against the moon. We had his whole upper body and head. The angle had distorted his proportions, and he appeared massive. His head was cocked, as if he listened intently, and his arms were bent, with his thick hands dangling down. He could have been preparing to plead or to pounce. His mouth was stretched open over long, gapping teeth, his bug eyes half-closed.

"Travis in ecstasy," I said, because the room was too hot and too quiet. Just as I spoke, Travis's face filled the screen, his eyes opening full, the dark irises steady and solid, and right toward us. The film ended then, though we had one more close-up of matted grass and dirt. The film flashed white and black and done.

We got the lights back on before Becky's father appeared again, and everyone looked unreal in that sudden brightness. The girls were pale, their lipsticked mouths full and garish. The guys seemed agitated, with no place to look. We split up to drive home. The guys piled into one car, the girls in another. The dips in the road were swirling with late-night fog, and we talked about how dangerous that was.

None of the girls spoke to Travis then; they even crossed the street to avoid passing him.

Someone must have mentioned the movie to the wrong person, because the film was taken from us—all our parents saw it, for sure. I know we all told the truth, that Travis had just been looking at lights until we came along. None of it was Travis's idea at all. But it didn't matter. He was too big, and he was changing. What if he went in someone's house now? Did we think he'd be satisfied with a quarter or something to eat? We didn't know. No one did, and no one was willing to risk finding out. People said something like him couldn't just be left loose, and since his parents hadn't been able to keep him in, there was no choice. Travis got taken to Sikeston.

The Sikeston house had trouble with him, too, or so we heard. He'd try to get out, and they had to lock him in a room by himself. One Saturday evening he did manage to leave. People said he broke a window or jim-mied it open, and crawled out into the dark. Sikeston is a much bigger town than the one we live in, with theaters and stores that stay open all night. Travis found himself an intersection. Two cars managed to miss him, but one jumped the curb and the driver got bruised pretty bad. People came out of restaurants, and someone took a picture that was in most local papers the next day. There was Travis, head back like a string was attached, hands up like some stupid puppy. He was dancing under what was probably a red light, and smiling in the middle of all that mess. The whole world got to see him in black and white. My mother cut the picture out and framed it and hung it in my room. "You think on this," she said.

They put Travis in Fielder a short time later. Once we all got together and wrote a letter to the institution people trying to explain how Travis felt about music and quarters and lights. The letter got too complicated, so we just wrote down the things he liked and taped some quarters to a piece of cardboard, wrote his name across the top, and mailed the whole thing off.

Then time passed, and we didn't talk about him anymore. We also quit hanging out at the bus station, not because of Travis, but because we sort of outgrew it and could go pretty much where we wanted. We would head for Dexter and drive around the one hangout, a barbecue place we called the Pit. We'd hoot and holler at Becky with one of her boyfriends, or we'd park next to a car full of boys from another town and smile at them till words were exchanged and a possible fight made someone have to go home.

Sometimes, though, we'd see someone who might be Travis, a strange boy with more muscles than brains, or with a lumbering walk in pants too short for the times, and one of us would say, "I wonder how Travis is." We'd joke about his having a room of his own with three flashing lights in the corner or having a job replacing neon bulbs at the Miss America pageant. Other times, we'd mention him and be quiet. Those were the nights when we drove through the countryside near Buxton, taking dirt roads around dead fields and talking about our girls or our futures. The night air would be heavy and moist, rolling through the window with years still to go. We'd be so full of hope and youth that we couldn't bear it, and there would be the moon, brimming full and bright, perfectly steady over all that land. We'd go silent then, ride for miles.

# ⠿ Pulse of the World ⠿

The older sister came home in August. It was truly a mad month, hot Missouri summer but no rain, so the grass dried and died and the wind swept maybe-moisture high up and past the little town. He had just turned sixteen and wanted a car worth driving. His younger sister, Ruth, ten, wanted to shave her legs. She wore a training bra beneath her cotton shirts, and he teased her about that. He had been, for two years, the oldest child in the house, and he liked it. He was tolerant with his little sister and deep voiced and calm with his mother. But he was adamant, too. He said cruel things in a casual way, winning her over with his young-man strength, with his father's curling smile over white, even teeth.

Then the big sister arrived with her baby in arms. They had to pick her up at the Poplar Bluff train depot, fifty-five miles away. She stepped down all wild haired and wide eyed, her new baby in the crook of her left arm. She wore jeans and was so thin they hung loosely about her hip bones. She hugged him with one arm, "God, you've grown," then turned to her sister. "Want to hold the baby?"

"No."

She laughed. "Neither did I." She kissed the forehead of the pale, tiny girl she held. "But now I do. Don't I? Yes, yes, I do." She glanced at all three of them. "You don't know how good it is to be here. I am so tired. So very tired."

He did the driving and felt quite separate from and superior to the women's talk. They steamed up the car, chattering. His sister smoked, and he thought about saying, "You shouldn't smoke with a baby," but he didn't want to break his own comfortable quiet. She was known for her retorts. Nothing got her down for long. That's what his mother said about her. "She'll always have a hard row to hoe, but it won't get her down. Nothing gets Cora down."

"So you're working," she said, and patted his thigh as if he weren't a grown man.

"Yeah."

Around them the hills flattened to gray cotton fields beneath a white clouded sky. As far as he could see, only poverty and labor, poor small-town boy domain, no money in his pockets, his mother's old car.

She took over the house, and that wasn't fair, though he didn't want to begrudge her. He knew she was about to go crazy, maybe had already done so, and everybody had to be easy with her. In the mornings now, when he returned from his job, she was still at the kitchen table, smoke billowing as if from her pores, coffee cup always at hand. He only worked till eight o'clock A.M., and by then his mother was gone to the factory.

"Looks like you could get a better job," his sister said,

clutching the baby up against her so it could see him, too. "Not that there's anything wrong with what you do, but you've always been so proud. And so clean. It must bother you."

"Oh, it bothers me," he said, and was grateful, momentarily, that she could see he shouldn't have to work at such a filthy job. He plucked chickens. It was ludicrous work, and nothing he wanted to own up to, but he wouldn't hide from it, either, especially around her. She had been the smart one. Was the smart one. But she was the one going crazy. She had come home because she was afraid she was going to hurt her baby.

"It scared me," he had overheard. "I woke up to her crying, and she seemed like a little wild animal to me. David was working nights, I wasn't getting any sleep, and she wouldn't nurse. She'd nurse a minute or two, then drop off. I tried flicking her feet, holding her nose, but she'd just cry and go to sleep the minute I stopped. Anyhow, with the lamp on, her shadow was on the wall, arms flailing. It really did look like an animal. I got scared I'd hurt her. The doctor said I'd used up all my reserve energy. Said I needed rest."

He wanted her to rest, but he wanted her to move, too. He wanted her to be neat and clean and sharp, to be evidence that out there was a better world.

"I got a new wardrobe," he told her the third morning.

"Show me," she said, all excited like it mattered. Her mood was contagious. He knew how nice he looked. Black shoes, black nylon socks that came up to just below his knees. Dark slacks, creased new and narrow. The shirts were solid colors, long sleeved with double wrist buttons. He saved the coat till last. A black trench coat, long and classic.

"Oh, sharp," she said. "Nice look."

He flipped it open. The lining was red.

"Perfect, James. Just like you. All quiet understatement but with fire on the inside."

He was so pleased it embarrassed him, and he took a long time putting his old clothes back on.

When he reemerged, she was gone. In the kitchen, Ruth was up, having toast. She wore a pink nightie and sat with her knees up to the table.

"Get some clothes on," he said.

"Make me."

He could see Cora through the window above the window fan. She was in a lawn chair at the end of the backyard. She was bending forward, elbows on knees, wrists pressed to her temples. He knew she was crying. He wished she had stayed in California with her husband. He walked down the hall to the front bedroom and pulled back the curtain that served as a door. The baby was on the folding bed in the corner. It was sleeping, he guessed. He thought mothers didn't leave new babies alone. The room smelled like milk and smoke. He started to open a window, but he thought he might wake up the baby, and besides, it wasn't his baby or his problem.

On Friday night and Saturday night, he took the car out by himself. "Going to Dexter," he said. He didn't, though. He was too ashamed of the car, but he wanted to establish his right to take it out on weekend nights. He drove north instead, up toward Bell City and Advance. He bought five candy bars and two Cokes at a little grocery and then parked on a gravel hill up from the drive-in. The moon was an orange circle above the screen. It rose gradually, and he got sadder. In a few weeks, he'd be back in school. He had nothing. His life was going to be the same. When he got home, the house was full of his two sisters. Smoke. Popcorn. A playpen filled the only clear space in the living room. The coffee table had been moved to the hallway.

"Where'd that come from?"

"She needs to be able to rest," his mother said. "She can't hold that baby every minute."

"It can't goddamn walk yet," he said.

"The folding bed isn't firm enough. She could smother."

"Let her," he said, and stalked to his room. He burned with the falseness of his last words. He didn't mean them. He just felt them. His shame forced him to storm back to the living room. He stopped at the end of hallway. "What I'd like to know is who paid for the damn thing."

"Watch your tone, James."

"I'm not gonna watch nothing. I buy my own clothes. We drive junk for a car, and you buy her a playpen for a kid that can't even play."

He thought he was at least witty. He turned away. He had to shoot one more time, just one more. "If you hadn't been so desperate for a man," he called, "maybe we'd have something." He slammed the door to his room and lay in the dark. He got thirsty but couldn't go after a drink. He fell asleep hot mouthed and hot minded. Once, vaguely, he heard the baby cry and wanted to yell something about that, too, but he fell back asleep.

When he came in from work the next morning, Cora was wiping down the kitchen cupboards.

"Hi, James," she said.

"Thought you were supposed to take it easy."

"Oh, I'm feeling better. Mom got up with Mary last night. I just needed sleep." She wadded the washcloth up in both hands. "Look. I know I've just sort of barged in again, and maybe you feel displaced."

"I don't feel displaced."

"Maybe you're angry with me."

"I'm not angry with anybody."

"You're mad at someone. Did you hear yourself last night?"

"I wasn't talking about you."

"Then that's worse. She's done the best she can. You can't talk that way to your own mother."

"Don't come in here telling me what I can and cannot say."

"So it is me."

"You're just like her. Get married to a no-good and want people to feel sorry for you."

"Go pluck chickens, kid. That's the kind of barnyard you belong in."

She turned her back on him then, and he hated the very squareness of her shoulders and the wild, bed-ragged curl of her hair. He picked up the saltshaker from the table and hurled it right at her spine, right at the center of the straight line that divided her self-right-eous shoulders. She grunted with the blow. She bowed her head, and he thought she might be crying, but he couldn't hear it. He waited for her to turn around so she could see that maybe he was sorry. She wouldn't. She always could do that, just be right when she was wrong.

"At least she married your dad before she got pregnant," he said.

She didn't respond.

When he turned toward the back room and bathroom, Ruth was leaning in the doorway. She had one foot drawn up, resting against the other knee. She had the baby over her shoulder. This sister was blond, with tear-drop, blue eyes.

"Slave labor," he said, and walked past her. Something made him stop and kiss the baby on the top of the head. His lips pressed against what he knew was the "soft spot" and it scared him, like he'd kissed a pulse of the world.

School started, but he didn't quit his job as he had promised. When he got home, he had ten minutes to shower and five to run across town. He left his dirty clothes on the bathroom floor, and sometime during the day they were washed and hung on the line. He removed his new clothing as soon as he came back in the afternoon. A few evenings he held the baby. Night fell earlier now, and the living room was closer. The lamps reflected in the windows like many rooms encircling this one, and though his anger seemed less, his despair seemed greater. He was in a maze of women, their rooms, their clothes, their hushed, lulling mother voices. He found bits of shaved hair clinging to the bathroom sink and rinsed it down cautiously, feeling that even conjecture was shameful. They were his sisters. Snow White and Rose Red. All thorny paths to doom.

Heating vents and thin walls disclosed more than he wanted to know the rest of his life. "James was a blue baby," his mother said. "I was afraid we'd lose him, so I was real careful with him. We spoiled him, I guess."

"We made him selfish, Mom. And you're not doing him any favors now."

"I know. But it's just a car. I mean, he's never had much. His dad never once checked on us, never wrote. Yours and Ruth's at least drops by from time to time. James has got to think about things like that. I'll get him a car, and maybe that'll turn the trick."

He wanted that car. He wanted that secret to spring out of them into his future, something he could be proud of, something that said he was more than a country kid, than an almost-bastard, a half-brother, not whole in any way. He didn't know how they could do it, but he wanted them to. He would accept the sacrifice. He would earn it even, with gratitude and softer ways. "You're a cute kid," he said to Ruth.

"I'm pretty," she said. "And I'm gonna be beautiful."

It was on a Saturday, just at lunch, that they finally mentioned the car aloud. His mother had fried bologna and fixed macaroni and cheese and green beans. He spread a thin layer of ketchup across the browned lunch meat, cut one thin wedge and rolled it. He liked eating in patterns; it was a poor man's style.

"You want to go look at cars, James?"

Inside he went rigid with yes, but he held his response so the delay would seem like surprise. He laid down his fork.

"Are you serious?"

"I talked with Mr. Welker at the bank. I think I can swing a better car. Nothing real fancy."

"Don't already say what it can't be. Just wait."

Cora got up to stand by the window. She lighted a cigarette. She'd wear jeans till she died, he supposed. She'd be buried in them, with a cigarette in each hand. With a cigarette in every orifice of her body.

"Eat your lunch," his mother said. "I should have waited to tell you. Eat. Then we can drive down to Dexter."

"How come he gets a car and I don't get anything?"

He squelched the blond rootling. "You haven't suffered yet," he said, and twisted the entire bologna slice into a tight roll. "Right, Momma? We have to earn our rewards in this family." He stuffed the roll into his mouth.

"Yours, I hope, is yet to come," Cora said.

He insisted they go to the Bluff, not to Dexter, because all the best buys were in the Bluff. Dealers there had more inroads from all the towns around here, got more trade-ins, and from people with more money, too. He'd know it the minute he saw it. He'd know it. Just exactly the right car for him.

"And you can't smoke in it," he said before he thought.

"Are you paying for it, brother?"

His mother sighed, a deep long exhalation he had heard too many times, and he could see without seeing how her back humped down and her head thrust forward, like an old turtle. He didn't know how two men had ever loved her, much less how one of them could have married her twice. Not his father, of course. Once

46

gone, he was forever gone. So here he, James, sat half-brother with two full-blood sisters. He had the car coming.

All the car lots had banners, red, blue, yellow streamers, and signs slashing prices on all their little lovely wonders. He coveted, he loved, he ached.

It was a black Mercury, with red interior. They all sat in it. He didn't want them to, but he didn't know how to stop it. They were rubbing off whatever newness was left. He was anxious to get it out of the lot, on the road, home, and to herd them into the house. They clashed terribly with the sleek beauty. He sped down the highway to music waved in from Chicago, rumbling basses and fast guitars.

"Slow down," his sister said, but he didn't.

"I'm going the speed limit."

"Then it's too fast."

Her red hair whipped across the lower part of her face.

She'd been beautiful a few years ago. She'd had the baby before the doctor could get there. The doctor had said, "You dropped that baby like a cow drops a calf." She had reported that to his mother, and had said it made her mad. "Made me sick. I'm not an animal. He made me feel like an animal."

Her husband hit her, too, every now and then. She was thinking about not going back. James knew all of this. And more. He knew she'd stood in a pan of hot water the night the baby was coming, and her husband had tried to shave her legs. He had cut the shin in such a long strip that it was still bleeding after the baby was born. He hadn't visited her for two days. When she went home, he hadn't thrown out the garbage, or made the bed, or even taken the dinner dishes from the table.

"I washed them the minute I got home," she had said.

He wished women didn't talk all the time, didn't fill every nook and cranny of every house and every breathing space with their secret sharings. He knew—though this he'd never overheard—he knew she'd find another man just as his mother had and another baby would come along, a little boy. They'd coax him and coo him and gobble him up.

Ruth leaned to the front seat. "Momma says for you to slow down. She's getting carsick."

He had to slow down then, had to creep along while they survived comfortably. On the last stretch, though, the few miles between Dexter and Buxton, he let her rip. He opened her up. The ladies screamed. Their hair waved and flapped like flags. The baby blanket blew open and fluttered around his sister's cheek.

"James! Goddamn it! James!" His sister, because his mother wouldn't use such language.

The fields ran flat and useless behind him, then rose gently, minutely, up toward Buxton. The water tower glinted in the fall sun, this little town proclaiming here, here, here we lie. He crowed, ecstatic, clean. He gunned toward the turnoff, to fly left, down, up toward the courthouse. He clipped the center median and the car skidded right, turned, bumped against the curb, over, bumped twice down, slid, stopped.

Silence.

In the mirror he saw his mother's profile. She seemed resting, thoughtful, as she often did before she spoke seriously to him. He heard Ruth begin whimpering, and his mother turned toward the sound. He was drawn to look at the sister beside him, but he delayed. He wasn't sure why. He knew she was unharmed. Something in the line of her jeaned leg and the hand that rested there assured him that if he did raise his gaze, he would meet her eyes. He wasn't ready. He himself wasn't hurt. He knew how he felt, but he wasn't ready yet to think about that, either.

Before him, down the embankment, a line of trees filtered the sudden slight breeze. They flickered different shades of green, turned dark from a cloud shadow. Something out of place lay on the ground near them. It was pink. A round lump. A striped blanket of something. He wasn't sure what. He wasn't yet sorry, but he still had years to turn and face his sister, the one who was going crazy, the one with stricken eyes. He was going to wait for a long time, maybe the rest of his life, because just now, in this moment, sitting between his past and his future, he felt absolutely and exactly right.

# ⊰ The Promise ⊱

The little girl was a fragile, pale thing, so naturally thin that her mother had a few times insisted that the doctor check her for anemia. "I don't," she had said, "want people thinking I don't cook good meals for the kids." Mary, the little girl, didn't want people thinking that, either. She knew she had a good mother. She liked her mother. Now, in the backseat of a Chevy station wagon, she breathed the smoke-laden air, avoided looking at her sister, and simply accepted her bodily misery as part of this childhood day. Her back ached; her stomach didn't feel right; she felt, vaguely, that she had to pee again although they had stopped at a gas station for her just a few moments ago. The hot desert sun slanted across her right forearm and right thigh, and she wanted to sit on the shady side of the seat, but her sister wouldn't change places. Mary wouldn't argue. She was nine years old and didn't want to be a whiner. No one liked whiners.

The car zoomed southeast, which all seemed downhill, nothing but cactus, dirt, rocks, sun. Mary was becoming accustomed to the desert. When they had first moved here, her mother called this country "foreign" and the "devil's own," and Mary had wanted to move back to her grandmother's country, with trees and water. Now, as the car exited the freeway, the road wound up a mountain and the air through the window whipped cool. Mary had cousins out here, and they would be at the festival. They were all blond, like her, but fatter and sassier. She liked every one of them, but they didn't like her much. She could tell. It was, her seven-year-old sister had explained, because Mary looked "like an angel." "You're too pretty to play with." Leslie had said that matter-of-factly but also longingly, and Mary hadn't known how to respond. "No, I'm not," she had said, because a person shouldn't be proud of being pretty. God made people pretty. And what God gave, God could take away.

"Doncha know," Mary now said aloud.

"Don't you know what?" from her mother.

"Nothing. I hope Aunt Bess is there."

"Oh, she'll be there. Her and her troop."

"I don't feel good," Mary said without planning to.

"Where do you feel bad?"

"All over."

Her mother turned sideways to lay one hand against Mary's cheek. "You are warm. But then, you've been sitting in the sun." She nudged Leslie's round, brown knee, and Leslie stirred from her half-sleep. "Change places with your sister for awhile."

Leslie complied, but in the exchange pushed her elbow into Mary's abdomen, and Mary thought she was going to wet her pants. "How much farther?" she said, but her mother had begun singing one of her favorite songs, and her father said, "Don't sing in the car. I don't know why you do that."

The road led down again, and the air turned warmer. It sang around the metal mirror, roared by Mary's face. She sat on the edge of the seat, but nothing helped much.

"Look," her mother said, pointing at the campground far below. "This is a big festival. God, I hope we don't have to walk far."

Mary, uneasy that her mother had said "God" so lightly, knew a festival wasn't a carnival. There would be no rides or games for kids, just a wooden stage, and tents where adults bought jewelry or instruments or music. Mary was familiar with festivals.

"I've gotta go to the bathroom," she said.

"We're almost there." Her mother's voice was excited, which made Mary hesitate to intrude again. Her mother never got to play much, and she loved to play. She had a beautiful voice. Mary was scared that she, herself, would never be able to sing but that Leslie would. Leslie didn't even try to practice or learn songs or listen to others, but sometimes her voice sounded just right, and Mary didn't know how Leslie did that. Leslie was sloppy and broke all the rules, but she didn't get punished much because she cried easily. Mary didn't understand that, either.

They couldn't find parking anywhere near the festival grounds and had to park partway up the mountain road. Her dad carried the ice chest. Mary was proud of the way he did it. He sat it on his left shoulder and carried two bags of supplies in his right arm. He was a short man, but he was very strong. He was a policeman, and good-looking. But he was also very quiet and usually mad at somebody, particularly her mother. Mary wanted him to have fun. She carried one sack and her mother's mandolin. Leslie carried the guitar case, but she couldn't carry it straight—her knees kept bumping it—so Mary gave Leslie one sack and took the guitar, too. Her mother, loaded with lawn chairs and potato salad, chattered all the way down, a constant pleasant humming sound that Mary knew was peacemaking, was trying to weave her father into this good day and this good time. Once he laughed, and Mary did, too, just in response.

When she went to look for the portable bathrooms, she had to go alone. The other kids were busy with a new slingshot and BB pellets. They claimed they hit the center of the target Bess had put up, but Mary thought there should be a sound, some kind of thump, and there was nothing. A bee followed her, and she worried it would get tangled up in her long hair and sting her. Sometimes people died from bee stings. She tried to walk straight and not dodge suddenly, because that might incite it to action. "Incite" was her father's latest word. He wasn't as smart as her mother, and he was always dropping new words around the house. Mary knew they laid traps for each other and then kissed because they felt ashamed of what they were doing most of the time.

The bathrooms were like gigantic bullet shells, silver metal with flat roofs. She had used similar ones before, at other festivals, and no longer worried about snakes being down there, or someone sneaking a look at her private parts. She still worried that the bathroom would topple over while her panties were down. But she couldn't pee much, and when she stopped trying, her body wrenched with such a chill that it frightened her. She felt like she was trying to turn inside out. She didn't want to pee any more this entire day. But she couldn't seem to stop trying. Someone banged on the door, and the metal clattered around her. She left, and in a few minutes felt better. She wasn't going back there. She'd wait till she got home to use the bathroom. Already, though, her body's need was urgent. Like her father's work was urgent. Dangerous. Important. Something her mother couldn't understand, as he said.

Mary wanted to join Bess's children, but instead she sat on a tree stump and held her knees up against her stomach. Her mother was now tuning up with Bess's husband. Her father was sitting at the base of a tree a few yards away, with a beer in one hand and a cigarette in another. He was watching her mother.

Once Leslie came loping over and said, "You sick or something?"

Mary shook her head.

"How come you're not playing?"

"I don't know."

"You look sick to me."

"I gotta pee all the time."

"You better tell Momma."

Her mother was now with a circle of musicians. A fiddler was tuning up, and her mother was nodding. "She's getting ready to go on, I think," Mary said.

"Tell Daddy."

He was still under the tree, but he was sleeping now, or pretending to. He slept a lot.

"No," Mary said. "I'm okay. But we should wake him up so he won't miss Momma on stage."

Leslie glanced toward their father. "I'm not gonna do it." She walked away. That, too, Leslie could do—stay out of their parents' war.

The next time Mary went to the bathroom, she hurt so bad she moaned. There was blood on the tissue. She was trembling. She couldn't get her panties up right. The waistband bunched over in back. She left it that way and went in search of her mother, or father, or Bess, or Leslie. Adults were everywhere, all different colors, tennis shoes, boots, hats, swirly skirts, shorts, brown legs. Her mother was coming down from the high, wooden stage. She wore jeans and a long-sleeved white blouse. Her hair was dark red, very long, and the wind whipped it. She looked like a stranger, maybe a woman from television. Mary had to walk in front of hundreds of people sitting on the ground before the stage. One woman had on a bathing suit and held a baby. Mary was glad her mother didn't dress that way. She trailed along behind her mother and the fiddler and Bess's husband.

"Mom," she said. "Mom."

The third time, her mother turned around. "There you are. Did you hear us play?"

Mary shook her head. She took her mother's hand and tugged.

When her mother finally got the message to step away from the men, Mary said, "I peed blood."

"You what?"

"When I peed, blood was on the paper."

"Oh, God." Her mother squatted down immediately, placed her palm on Mary's cheek. "You're burning up." She stood up, muttering "God" again, and talking about being so damned ashamed of herself. "I don't listen, do I, baby? Damn. We'll go back right now. You should have told me, Mary. Why do you do that? You don't have to be a martyr, honey. You're a kid. I'm so damned ashamed of myself." A few yards on, by some musicians who called "Good job," "Hot set," Mary's mother said, "And is your dad going to be mad. He finally comes and here I go, goofing up again." She tried to carry Mary the rest of the way, but she had to put her down. "I can't do anything right, can I?"

When her mother talked to Bess, the kids gradually stopped playing, stood all alert and quick eyed nearer and nearer the adults. They studied Mary, and she tried to be as somber as this early departure merited. Bess gave her a huge paper cup filled with ice water. "You keep drinking, Mary, until you see a doctor. No sodas, just water. Okay? That'll help right away." Mary wished Bess could come with them.

Her father made two trips so he could carry her to the car. On the way back, with the sun steaming through the front window, he said, "Jesus, Cora. Don't you ever listen to the kid?" He only spoke once more the entire ninety miles. "Mary, if you need me to stop, you just say so. Don't hesitate at all. Got me?" He caught her gaze in the mirror. Mary nodded. Then she waited for him at least to look toward her mother, but he didn't. She believed he had meant what he said, but still, she was afraid to interrupt his anger. She held her pain.

"Pop," Leslie blurted, and tapped him on the shoulder. "I need a gas station."

Leslie went in with Mary. She said, "I don't want to see any blood." A moment later, she added, "I hope I don't get it."

In town, at the emergency room, Mary had to pee into a little jar that her mother held. It hurt so much that she

twisted her body against the sick pain, and groaned, just
a little. When she stood, she saw that blood had come
from her into the jar. "Oh, God," her mother said. "I
am so sorry."

Mary assumed that she was dying.

The specialist doctor explained the test procedure to
both Mary and her mother. He drew a picture of a tiny
balloon and a skinny pipe that was part of Mary's body.
He planned to let the balloon float loose in Mary's body,
like it was the sky, like it was something anyone could
use.

"No," Mary said, and folded her thin arms across her
midriff. She had on just a blue print housecoat, open in
the back. Her legs from the knees down dangled from
the table, and they had turned bluish. That frightened
her and embarrassed her. They looked ugly. The blond
hairs were prominent, and the scar on her right kneecap
looked larger. Her middle toe was longer than the big
one, and that meant she was bossy, her grandmother
Oida had said. She didn't want people to know things
about her without her consent.

"It'll be slightly uncomfortable, but it won't hurt."

She didn't like this doctor. He had a thick, long
beard, and eyes as black as raisins. His eyeteeth were
crooked and lapped toward the center. He had a wiry
voice, all high and whiny: "Now Mary . . . now Mary."

"Honey," her mother said. "You've gotta have it
done, or you'll get one infection right after the other."

Her mother's teeth were even and white. Her eyes
were blue. She was a very pretty woman, but she only said

"baby," "sugar," "honey," when Leslie or Mary got sick, and now she kept saying such words. Each one wrapped Mary in misery. She had no choice.

"No shots," she bartered.

The doctor raised one crooked finger. "One," he said. "We'll have to give you one shot so you'll be comfortable. That's it."

Mary held her silence for a few minutes. Then she breathed "okay" and looked to her mother.

The test hurt. After it was over and the balloon had floated down to hell and Mary had ridden home with her parents, she said, "It hurt," three different times. She clipped the words really short and sharp, but not with any expectation that anyone could undo what was done. She wasn't going to let them touch her again. Never.

Then the doctor called them in and drew pictures of a valve in Mary's body. He drew a thin pipe to it and a thin pipe out of it. "The valve won't close," he said. "So the urine backs up into the kidney. If we don't correct this now, infections could damage her kidneys permanently."

"No," Mary said, before they asked her anything at all. She was naked beneath the robe. She pressed her skinny legs together as tightly as she could. The doctor and her mother were telling her how easy and fast it would be.

"Only one shot at the hospital, too," the doctor said. "And you'll be asleep, all better, and home again."

Mary held up one straight finger. "No more." Her voice was sharp, like a bark. It embarrassed her a little, but she wanted out of there. She shook her head rapidly against whatever they were thinking and felt her hair brush her cheeks like a gentle touch.

Later, she overheard her mother on the phone. "I'm sort of proud of her. She knows how to stick up for herself."

Mary didn't want to stick up for herself, and now she had to.

Mary was in a large room with four beds, all but hers empty. Her father was in the waiting room because he didn't like hospitals and he wanted Mary to "have her privacy." Her mother stood by the windows that spanned one wall. Outside, the sun shone. In the far distance was a mountain. Mary recalled its name. "A" mountain. Like it was the first.

A man in a white coat and pants came in. "Hey, Mary. How you doing?" He pulled a rolling stool up to the bed and took her left hand.

She drew it back.

He took her fingers, tugged lightly. "Gotta get a blood sample, Mary. One little sting and that's it. Over before you know it."

This was the one shot, then, what they'd agreed to. Mary eased her resistance, let him draw her hand forward. Her mother had neared the bed, stood watching. Her mother wore jeans and a white shirt. She looked different here, with all the steel and white; she looked maybe a little dirty.

"Good girl," he said, and twisted a bandage over the tip of her finger. He spun the stool away toward the corner and left.

Her mother touched her forehead. "You were good," she said. "This won't take long, hon. Then we'll be home, you'll be fine, and no more doctors."

A smear of blood edged out from the Band-Aid. "I need a Kleenex," Mary said. Her mother brought a piece of toilet paper from the bathroom.

A man and a woman, both nurses, came into the room. They stood on either side of the bed. The woman was holding a needle.

"I already had a shot," Mary said, and sat up straight. "He said one shot, Momma." She looked at her mother.

"That wasn't a shot, hon. He just took a blood sample."

Mary started to get down from the bed. The man grasped her arm, not hard, and pushed her back. She leaned against him, as heavy as she could make herself. "He promised one shot," she said. When the woman took her other arm, she threw herself from side to side, screeched, "One, one, one." The man held her against the bed, and the woman left the room. Mary tried to squirm, but he pressed down so her arms hurt. Her robe had twisted up. She wrapped one skinny leg around the other, trying to make a knot of herself.

The woman nurse came back with the doctor.

"Now, Mary," he said sternly, his crooked teeth and solid black beard ugly and foreign. "You know that wasn't a shot. You're not living up to your part of the bargain."

"You promised one shot."

"That wasn't a shot."

"You promised one shot."

The three of them held her down. She could see her

mother's jeans and white shirt through the angles of their arms. Her father was still somewhere else. He could kill people if he wanted to. The room got dreamy and underwater, and she hoped this was dying because it was pleasant, like someone loved her.

When she woke, she hurt. She had to pee. Something was between her legs. She fumbled up the gown and put her hand down there. It came up bloody again. Was she still sick? She tried to sit up, then did. And there was her mother. "Mary, lie down, baby. Don't sit up. What do you want, honey?"

"I got to go to the bathroom."

"They'll bring you a pan. You lie back. Lie back."

She pushed her mother's hand away. "I gotta wash off the blood. It's getting on the sheets."

Her mother gripped her arm, but she let go when Mary began struggling. "Don't thrash around, honey. Please. Lie still. Nurse!" Her mother ran toward the door. "Goddamn it! Nurse!"

Mary wasn't staying here. Getting down from the bed was difficult, though, too slow. When she did stand free, her knees buckled, and she fell. Then she worried she'd get blood on their floor, so she clasped both her hands between her legs.

Her mother was back, scooped her up in both arms like Mary was just a baby. "Get somebody in here," she screamed. "And get her a pad, for God's sake. She's a proud kid." She laid Mary back on the bed. "You just bleed all over their sheets, baby. Don't give a damn about any of them."

"They said one shot."

Her father came into the room later, in uniform. She

thought he might do something, though she couldn't imagine what. She wanted the doctor to see her father with his gun and badge, but he didn't seem impressed. He said, "She's fine, or will be. It's a simple procedure, really. She should be okay from now on." He looked at Mary then.

"I'm gonna sue you when I grow up," Mary said.

He took both her parents out in the hall.

Her father came in first. He picked Mary up in both his arms and said, "You need to be home."

They waited in the car for just a few minutes. The afternoon was breathless hot. No one should live in a desert. There were no rivers. It might never rain, never. Her father reached over the seat to pat her knee. Mary wanted to grab the hand and keep it right there by her forever. Her mother came out, and Mary remembered how beautiful her mother was sometimes, especially when singing. Her mother turned sideways to keep one hand on Mary all the way home. Both parents loved her, Mary knew.

"That doctor's an idiot," the mother said. "Antisocial. He says she's antisocial. Can you believe the bastard?"

Mary cringed because maybe the word "bastard" would cause her more pain. She couldn't learn fast enough to be safe.

"He screwed up," her father said. "He broke his promise, and he didn't want to own up. She called him on it."

They put her in her own bed and phoned the neighbors to send Leslie on down. Leslie padded in all freckled and dark haired, like a cherub on a funny Christmas card. "Did it hurt?" she said.

Mary nodded. "I won't ever go to a doctor again."

"You will if Momma says."

Mary watched Leslie's mouth. It was moist, shaped like a doll's. It was outlined in brown, like chocolate. "No," she said. "I won't."

She fell asleep. She didn't remember Leslie leaving. She woke to a dark room, with a patch of night sky showing through the high window. From the family room came the muted sounds of television gunfire. Her father would be watching. Softer, from somewhere else, came hushed guitar strings and her mother's evening voice. Mary lay in mild ache, listening, waiting. She heard Leslie's quick laughter from outside, followed by ripples from other children, all playing late. But that still wasn't all. Something else should speak, should make itself known. It was that something that could make her safe forever or never safe at all. Mary fought her body's need to rest and heal. She stared at the night window until stars took shape and she could at least make them into a dome, something all around the world, held there by her fierce determination alone.

# A Winter Snake

The woodpile had been in the alley behind the Good
Food Cafe for at least two years, since the owner cut
down the three trees that might shield a rapist or mur-
derer, although no one had, to anyone's knowledge,
been raped in Buxton or actually murdered. There was
some speculation that a woman whose body had been
found in the marsh east of town, her face in a shallow
pool, had not stumbled out of her house in a drug-
induced delirium, but had been carried there by her
husband. That was only speculation, though, and cut-
ting down the trees behind the cafe wouldn't have made
that outcome different anyway.

This particular day was a brown, cloudy one, when the
near-winter sky wouldn't rain and wouldn't clear, but
hovered and occasionally blustered a cold wind and a few
spirals of leaves. Down the alley came Martha Weaver.
She worked for the prosecuting attorney of Green
County, and had given up a job in the factory to earn
only one-third as much for typing a few forms a day. She
hadn't yet been able to explain why to anyone's satisfac-
tion. She was a skinny young woman, fine boned and

tall, with tear-drop eyes and long curly hair she wouldn't let curl. She brushed it hard straight, wet it down, and fashioned a long roll that she pinned up the center-back of her head. Her young husband, a man who liked pool and the guys, was overseas, and Martha spent most of her time being faithful to him. This wasn't easy, since a state trooper came in the prosecuting attorney's office regularly and made the same remark a number of ways, about Martha letting her hair down.

Just as Martha was passing the woodpile, trying to keep her black high heels from sinking into the mud, it came to her that a snake could have slithered under there. She could visualize the snake, a thick one, jet black and fat, sluggish, crawling under the chopped limbs almost before her eyes. That gave her the shivers so that she hurried past and believed she saw the narrow tip of the snake's tail wriggle the last inch away. She clicked onto the sidewalk, around the corner, through the glass-paned door, and into Buxton lunch hour at its only real cafe. She sat at the last table ever taken, the one by the door, where the chill would sweep in with each person coming and going, and picked up the red plastic menu.

When the waitress stopped, Martha intended to say she wanted the special, chicken and dumplings, but instead she said, "I just saw a snake crawl under the woodpile out back."

"No."

"Yes, I did." Martha was going to add that it was only a black snake, but the waitress was already calling, "Jim! Hey, Jim, Martha says she saw a snake in the alley, crawled under the woodpile." She turned back to Martha. "You sure? Maybe you saw a stick."

65

"I know a snake from a stick," Martha said.

The owner, Jim, was already taking off his apron, and two people, both men, had called from their red-checkered table. "You're not scared of snakes are you, Martha?" from one, and, "You'd better tell your boss. Must be against the law for a snake to be out in November."

Martha had forgotten about that, that snakes weren't out in the winter. But then, a woodpile would keep a snake warm, or might. She didn't know.

"Harold wouldn't tease me," she said to the man who wouldn't take his cap off in the cafe, "and he wouldn't keep his hat on in a restaurant, either."

Now Jim had his coat on and wanted Martha to show him "where it went."

She didn't want to do that, but she had no choice. Half the people in the room were standing up and putting on their coats or already heading out the back door. She had only an hour for lunch, and she wouldn't have time to eat if they messed around too long.

"Let it go," she told Jim. "It was just a black snake."

He wasn't going to let it go, though, and she had to put her coat back on and face the wind, then walk on her tiptoes in the muddy alley to save her heels.

"Right there," she said and pointed at the end of the stack nearest the back door. "He went from that block, right across here, and right under that cracked log."

Jim was tossing logs to the other side of the door. Then two other men were starting, farther down the pile.

"Somebody watch that end," Jim said. "If he comes out, get him."

"With what?"

"Get a hoe," somebody said.

"A shovel would do. You got a shovel, Jim?"

Two women from the cafe had come around to the alley, and they stood on the other side from Martha. Martha thrust her hands in her pockets. She didn't know why she had said it about the snake, but it wasn't anybody's business. There could be a snake under there. She hoped one came running out. But even if it didn't, it could have gone anywhere by now. She was in that restaurant long enough.

"It could've gone anywhere," she said. "Let's just go back in. My lunch hour will be gone."

"Not anyplace it could go. We'll get him. Any minute now."

"Well, I'm going to have my lunch," Martha said.

She thought the ladies were talking about her, so she smiled at them, and shrugged, like men were crazy and what could she do about it? One of them smiled back, but it wasn't a genuine smile. Martha had lived here all her life, and that smile was a sick we-know-you smile.

When she went around the corner again, she said a quick little prayer. "Let a snake be under there, even if he's dead."

Inside the cafe, she went back to the counter and said, "Could you get me some chicken and dumplings to go? I've got to get back."

"They got that snake yet?"

"That snake could be anywhere by now. I haven't got time for such foolishness."

She was afraid they'd come back in before she got her takeout package, and she was right. She had to pass the two women and the man with the baseball cap.

"There wasn't no snake back there, Martha," the man said. "What you doing telling a crazy thing like that?"

"The fact that you can't find it, Mister, doesn't mean I didn't see it." She flounced out without looking at the women.

She had to take the long way back to work, to avoid the alley, and she wondered why, why, why, Lordy, did she say that about the goddamned snake? She felt so stupid, so ridiculous. And why couldn't there have been one under there? What law of nature couldn't make a snake appear when one was needed since they appeared so godawful often when they weren't?

In the office, she hung up her coat and went to the bathroom for some paper towels to put on her desk.

"That was a quick lunch," her boss said when she passed his doorway.

"Those fools over there," she tossed over her shoulder. "I didn't want to stay." She felt as if he already knew the whole story. She got the towels and saw how flushed her cheeks were. She rinsed them in cold water for a few minutes. On her way back, she paused by his office. She wanted to tell him she'd just told a lie, and have him laugh and make a joke out of it. "I saw a snake in the alley, and they make this big to-do about it, and when they can't find it, they act like I made up the whole tale. Who would do that?" she said. "Why would anyone say they'd seen a snake if they hadn't? They're a bunch of know-it-alls." She turned away before he could respond. "They make me sick," she muttered.

She was so choked up then, she didn't want to eat, but she took a mouthful anyway, and then couldn't swallow it. She sat there feeling like she might cry but trying not to long enough to get the food down her throat.

Her boss appeared in the doorway. "Did you really see a snake, Martha?"

Then she did cry, and dumpling juice dripped onto her best, only, dark blue dress.

"I'm sorry," he said, and went back in his office.

Then he looked at her funny all afternoon. She swore he did. He called her in and handed her one of his thick books with the white slips of paper marking pages.

"Only four paragraphs apply, Martha. Just type them as they are."

He was a pale-skinned, pink-lipped man, with hips wider than her own. His wife was all crippled with something, and her skin so dried up it flaked through her black stockings when she came to the office. He had done that to his wife, Martha knew, just as sure as she knew he probably kissed with his mouth closed. Martha had gotten the job by calling him back after her interview and saying, "I'll work really hard if you hire me. I just want a job commiserate with my abilities." Two weeks after he hired her, he laid a dictionary on her desk with two words marked by paperclips, "commensurate" and "commiserate." He had been teasing, she knew, because he wasn't an unkind man, but she hated that memory.

Now she took his blasted book and cleared her desk of the paper towels. She threw away the dumplings, wasting good money when she had precious little. She tried wiping the stain from her dress, but the wet paper towels left white fuzz, and that looked worse than the stain.

She had no sooner started typing than Jim from the

cafe called. "Did you really see a snake out there, Martha? I got to know."

"You don't want the truth, Mister," Martha said. "I gave that to you. You want a lie, so I'll give that to you. No, I didn't see no snake. I made it up so I could stand out in the cold and be treated like a fool by everybody. I told you to let the damned thing go, but would you do it? No. You had to keep stirring up that damn woodpile."

"But you really did see one?"

"I really did see one," she said. "And I'm glad the son of a bitch got away."

The sections she was copying from the book were about bestiality. She knew what that was no matter how the words tried to skirt it. She just wondered what kind of animal this Hiram Lawson had done it with, and most of all, who turned him in? Usually, she could ask questions about cases, but not about one like this. She knew better.

When she took him the typed complaint, she said, "You going for lunch? They got good specials today." She regretted it the moment she said it, because he would hear what they had to say about the snake. "It's cold out, though," she said. "Real sharp wind."

She typed the bad-check list for the local newspaper and was feeling almost back to normal when her boss came out of his office with his coat on. "I'm going to run this over to the courthouse and stop for some lunch," he said. He took the file with him.

She checked his desk, just to make sure, but there wasn't a thing on that Hiram Lawson. She got vinegar from the storage cabinet and washed the inside of the front window. Harold wanted her to stay busy at something all the time. When she saw him coming back, she went outside and began washing there.

"Too cold to be doing that, isn't it?" he said.

"Needs it," she said back, and he went on in, without telling her to let the windows go. Then she had to finish, and her hands were already almost numb.

When the trooper came by, it was just half an hour short of quitting time. He winked at her. "Got to talk to Harold," he said, "but don't take off before I come back out."

"If it's five, I'm gone," she said. "I've ruined a dress and washed windows, and that's a day's worth of labor anywhere."

She rolled her chair to face the window and watched the main street of Buxton. No one was on the sidewalks. The Western Auto had two tires on display, and they'd been there for at least nine months, as long as she'd had this job. Her husband had been gone for a year, had six months to go, and had written her twelve letters, all with SWAK penciled on the outside. He wrote everything in pencil, and she'd smudged most of it away by reading the letters every night and sleeping with them under her pillow or beside her. Her husband was going to be a mechanic when he came back.

Each time she looked at the clock, it was only a minute past the time before.

The men came out together, and she covered the typewriter. The trooper pulled one of the waiting chairs up next to her desk.

"Think I'll visit with Martha awhile," he said.

Her boss left, all bundled up in a heavy coat, wearing a hat.

"You seen his wife lately?" Martha asked, still looking out the window, watching the dark coat disappear around the corner. "She's worse every month."

"Hear you stirred up the cafe today. Something about a big, thick snake."

"You go to hell."

He had scooted his chair around to block her at her desk.

"You didn't see no snake," he said. "You're bored." He put one heavy hand on her knee, and Martha brushed it away.

"Keep thinking it'll rain or something," she said. "Just threatens all the time."

He grasped the arm of her chair and turned her to him. He put one hand on each of her thighs and slid them up till his thumbs were at her groin.

"I'm not threatening. I'm offering."

"Leave me alone."

"You don't mean that."

"Don't tell me what I mean." She tried to stand up, but he held her firm.

"Let's just go for a drink," he said.

"I don't drink."

"Of course you don't."

"And I don't fool around, either."

"I know that. Everybody knows that."

She felt flustered, angry. "Nobody knows anything about me," she said. She looked at his big hands on her legs, then at him. He was smiling. "Look, buddy," she said, "I can fill out a complaint as well as type them."

He hesitated.

"And I can call the sheriff's office, too," she said.

He lifted his hands straight up, palms out. "If you change your mind, honey."

"I won't tell you."

She cleaned off the top of her desk till he was out the door and watched him drive away.

"I got to go home," she said to the empty office. She went down the hall for her coat. "Though Lord knows why."

She drove past the cafe. The trooper's car was parked in front. She could see a few people seated at the tables, all men. She wanted to go in there right now, this very minute, show them. But she guessed she wouldn't eat in there for a few weeks. She'd bring her lunch from home. At the end of the block, she turned right and then right again.

She stopped by the back entrance to the cafe. Wood chips lay scattered all across the ground, the wood now divided into two piles. She studied the bottom logs, the dark recesses between them. She got out of the car and walked to the stacks. She shivered. She bent down.

"You under there?" she whispered. "I bet you are. Well, let me tell you something." She raised up, rested her weight on her heels. She spoke more firmly, toward the woodpile and toward the restaurant beyond. "I'll tell you what. If you ever do come out, I'm going to kill you myself."

# ⊰Searching for Heroes⊱

Buxton High School sat on a hill just west of the factory. It was a brick building, very old, and somehow stark in spite of the years of young people who had passed through it and on out of Buxton. The teachers there were of two kinds: hardy and long-time residents of Buxton, or young and desperate to leave before time found them forever rooted in a town totally barren and defiant of modern ways. The teachers had dealt with many problems common to a small rural town, perhaps common to any town. They had engaged in hushed discussions of a young girl who was pregnant by her father, whose case was pending in court docket. They had confronted a drinking mother over the bruises her children couldn't hide. They had led a boy from class knowing he had to face the sudden, accidental death of his father from a rolling tractor. But they had never encountered a problem such as Buddy Underwood.

Buddy and his sister entered the school the same fall, coming from a one-room school near Elm Ridge. He was the older, but had been held back for some reason. No word preceded him, about either his scholastic abil-

ity or his nature. This was in contrast to the town children, whose possibilities were well-known before their
faces. The new children, the Underwoods, appeared to
be from poor stock, but clean and neat. They were
brown skinned, round muscled, with similar hair—
short, thick, and lustrous, cut in a bowl style. The girl
was nice enough, very polite and soft-spoken, even
attractive if a person looked at her features. And she was
attentive and responsive in classes. Not so, Buddy.
Without speaking at all, he managed to disrupt every
class he was in.

Phil Weber noticed Buddy's actions first. It was the
second week of the fall semester, and classes still hadn't
settled down. The windows were open, and the warm fall
day was filled with sounds of birds and the occasional
whine of a car. Someone in the room whispered, "My
God," and a girl tittered. Phil couldn't tell which two
had vocalized such interest, but he glanced across the
room and saw Kay Miller shielding the right side of her
face, obviously blocking the placid profile of Buddy
Underwood.

"Did I miss something?" Phil said, and sat easily on
the corner of his desk. "Want to fill me in?"

No one spoke. Many students avoided his gaze. Phil
continued his explanation of paragraphing, but he kept
an eye on Kay Miller. She dropped her hand once, then
immediately shielded her face again. Phil casually walked
to the head of her row, all the while assigning a brief
exercise. He could see the length of the aisle between
Kay and Buddy, and nothing evidenced itself—no paper,
rubber band, food.

"So," Phil said, as if totally focused on teaching, "do

you understand? For the next few minutes, write, write, write. Make it interesting."

"Oh, it's interesting," a voice muttered.

"Write," Phil said, but he walked toward the boy, whose voice he recognized. He bent down. "What's going on?"

"That new kid."

"I know that. What about him?"

"Nothing."

"Come on, now. No game playing. What is it?"

"What he's doing."

Phil glanced at Buddy. He wasn't writing. He was staring straight ahead.

"I don't see anything."

The boy shrugged, straightened his paper.

Phil left him alone. He strolled up each aisle. At Buddy's desk, he stopped, but Buddy didn't look up. "You're not writing. Get some paper out. Participate."

Buddy giggled. It was a liquid giggle, as though he had not swallowed in quite a while.

Now the whole class was watching, including the ostensibly repulsed Kay Miller, so Phil followed her eyes.

Buddy was fondling himself. His left hand was in his pocket, but he was obviously massaging his groin.

"Keep writing," Phil barked, and walked back to the blackboard, as if Buddy, too, had complied.

Just before time for the bell, Phil positioned himself by the door, casually strolling out first as if to monitor the hall. When Buddy exited, Phil touched his arm.

"I'd like to speak with you a minute." He was very direct, as he believed teachers should be. "Your behavior in class was inappropriate. I don't want to see that happening again."

Buddy giggled. Phil felt instant repulsion.

"I mean it. I'll send you to the office. Okay? This is the only warning."

"Okay." The boy walked away like any healthy farm boy, easily and strongly. Phil found that disconcerting. The in-class behavior suggested something distasteful, but Buddy didn't look abnormal.

The next day it happened again. The heat of dead-calm late summer infiltrated the room. Students sweated, chewed gum, read aloud, tore paper from notebooks. But expectation hung in the room like humidity. Phil knew Buddy was doing it again just from the attitude of the students. They weren't hiding their faces now. They were raising brows at one another, grimacing, as if once aware, they had become in-group superior, both to Buddy and to Phil. They were, however, scrupulously attentive to their work, as if that wall of solidarity helped keep them separate from Buddy.

Phil walked to the doorway of the classroom. All eyes watched him.

"Buddy," he said. "Would you come in the hall with me, please?"

Buddy stayed where he was. His brown eyes swept to Phil, then away. He stared at the blackboard.

"Buddy. Get up, get your books, and come into the hall."

He seemed to think about it. His mouth was slightly open, too moist, and his eyes darted again to Phil. Then he scooted out slowly, took his books from the bottom

77

space of the desk, and walked up the aisle. The girls leaned away from him.

"Keep it down in here," Phil said, and a guffaw followed by "Tell Buddy that!" made him smile, too, but only for a moment. He followed Buddy out and closed the door behind them. "I told you that had to stop. You can't behave like that in my class. Any class."

Buddy, mute and patient, waited with each hand in a pants pocket, but the hands were, to Phil's relief, still.

"So. Okay. Let's go to the office. You can talk to the principal." Phil started down the hall, fully expecting that Buddy would follow. When he realized the boy wasn't with him, he turned. Buddy was at the top of the stairway, then going down to the second floor.

"Buddy Underwood!"

Buddy continued on.

Two students appeared in the doorway, Miles Barter and Larry Becraft, both town boys and good students.

"Get back in there. This doesn't concern you." Phil adopted the attitude that nothing unusual had happened.

Within a few days, almost everyone knew about Buddy. The students watched him from small groups, the girls forming circles, the boys half-moons. Two or three of the rougher male students called to Buddy. "You ever shift into high speed, Buddy?" "Hear you're afraid of heights, Buddy. Have to hang on to something to stay in your chair?" A few boys even nodded to Buddy in the hallway. But most were quiet about it. They watched him closely, worried about him. They were both disappointed and relieved that in the PE classes, Buddy did exactly as he was told. He was quick on his feet, a little awkward but quick to learn in basketball. They were also relieved that in the gym locker room, Buddy wrapped himself in a towel, and that the showers were themselves outdated, each with a separate concrete partition.

Buddy didn't offer conversation but would return greetings with a "Hey," or "Howya doing," or an occasional "Hot damn," which served as a compliment for a good play.

The young men considered a defense. "His pants are just too tight," Wayne Tilley offered. "He's adjusting himself."

"Bullshit."

"He's got some kind of medical condition."

"It's a condition, okay. I get it, too."

Two other teachers tried to make Buddy leave their rooms, but in one class Buddy ignored the request. The principal was sent for. Mr. Berman came into the room, bent down by Buddy's desk, whispered, and finally just seized Buddy by the arm and tried to lift him. Buddy wrapped the toe part of each foot around the front chair legs, removed his hand from his pocket, and held onto the flat desktop. The chair slid on the concrete floor, then tilted over, fell, and Buddy banged his head on the floor.

"You all right?" the principal said. "Young man?" He bent, since he was too heavy and old to kneel easily. "Young man?" Buddy's eyes were open and rolled toward Mr. Berman like the eyes of a dog temporarily down but far from cowed. Mr. Berman had two students right the chair since Buddy wouldn't move, and then he checked the left side of Buddy's head. "You've got a nasty bump here. I'll call your parents."

The parents didn't have a phone on record. The address was rural. Principal Berman sent a note to the classroom to be given to Buddy. It told him he could be excused from classes today if he had a way home. Buddy didn't leave at all. He sat in the same position until the bell rang, then went on to his next class. Two hours later, another teacher asked Buddy to go to the office, and, as he had with Phil Weber, Buddy left the building. Some students saw him before dismissal time, sitting under the one shade tree, facing the factory and drinking a soda. When the final bell rang, he stood up and faced the building. Miles Barter and Larry Becraft walked down the slope.

"You okay?" Larry said. "You could've cracked your head wide open."

"I'm okay," Buddy said. He had that deep voice Phil had noticed, but it was also mushy, as if he didn't close his lips tightly. Still, if he hadn't giggled, they would have thought he was almost a regular guy.

"You ought to cut that crap out in class," Miles said.

Buddy didn't respond, but he didn't turn away, either. He met Miles's eyes, which Miles later said gave him the willies. He didn't know what disturbed him.

Miles and Larry walked on toward the factory. When they glanced back, Buddy had been joined by his sister.

Later, one of the girls mentioned that Buddy's eyes floated, the dark irises highlighted by the white underneath them.

"That's why he looks loony," Miles said. "Got a retard's eyes."

"Got slut's eyes," Larry corrected. "Those are girl's eyes."

Larry was sorry he'd said that, because Miles was obviously making something of it.

Mr. Berman waited outside Buddy's last class one Tuesday. "You are suspended until you can behave as you should in the classroom. I've written your parents and advised them that you may not return here until they can assure me that you will act appropriately."

The next day, Buddy appeared in his first class, a study hall, at exactly seven forty-five A.M. He opened a math book and occasionally turned pages with his right hand. His left hand was in his pocket. Mrs. Hawkins left her desk long enough to stride down the hall, open the door to the principal's office, and say, "Buddy Underwood's in my study hall going about his business."

The next teachers' meeting focused on the problem of Buddy Underwood. It was early morning in mid-October. The one tree in front of the school was still bursting orange, but the sky was almost wintry. Teachers were cold and pressed for time, and they felt dealing with Buddy was Mr. Berman's domain, and he wasn't doing his job. He reported that he had written the parents to come in for a conference, but had had no response. He had called Buddy's sister into the office, and had sent a note home with her, too. When asked, she said the parents had read the note and she didn't know why they didn't come in.

"I advised her," Mr. Berman said, "that I would have

to come to their home if they didn't contact me. That was two weeks ago. I want two of you to go with me. This is the kind of situation that requires witnesses."

"Maybe," Lila Murphy said, "we should just ignore the kid. He took a test for me this week. It's the first work he's done. He apparently listens, because he scored well, in the high nineties. He can apparently read and write."

The art teacher reported that Buddy would draw, too. "Some things he won't do, and some he will. Maybe Lila's right."

Mr. Berman thought that even if they decided to ignore Buddy, someone still needed to speak with the parents and perhaps check on the living conditions. He could, of course, ask the sheriff's office to send somebody out there, but then it would appear in the sheriff's reports in the local newspaper, and surely that should be avoided.

Phil Weber and Lila Murphy rode along. They were two of the youngest teachers, Phil from a northern state, and Lila from somewhere in the Southwest. They were both blond and slender.

"He needs counseling," Lila said. "If we had a counselor, he'd at least know the proper authorities to contact. There have to be some channels. This school district is way behind the times."

"They don't have channels here," Phil responded. "Maybe we're just making too much of the whole thing."

"Not if he needs help."

Outside the car, the flatlands were bare of crops that had been sparse at best. Occasional houses centered acres of gray land, the soil clumped and hard. Mr. Berman smoked, kept the window partway open. Phil Weber sat in the backseat and admired the uniform blondness of Lila's hair. He tapped the window with his knuckle.

"I asked my doctor about Buddy. He said the boy probably needs counseling, but we may just make it worse if we try to correct him. So maybe we would do better to ignore it, like Lila suggested. All the kids seem to have adjusted."

"Could we do that?" Lila asked. "Let it slide?"

Mr. Berman thought so. "Or we could bring it up to the school board."

"That'd be something, wouldn't it?" Phil leaned forward. "Would that make the school board news in the paper?" He and Lila laughed slightly, then just watched the bleak scenery.

The Underwood place was six miles from the main road and a mile from the rural turnoff. Three mailboxes indicated that other families lived in the same area, but only one box had a name painted on the gray metal. "Underwood" had been carefully blocked in black on each side, just under the rural number. On the front, centered beneath the pull latch, was a hand-painted bouquet of delicate yellow flowers.

"Can't be all bad," Lila said.

If the house had ever been painted, no sign was left. The rough, splintery boards were black with a tar seal. The front porch sloped as if it had been built to shed rain from the house. But the place was as neat as a dirt yard in flatland could be. Thin swirls from a fine rake or a crude broom marked the yard area. Someone had swept or raked recently. Under a lean-to near the back sat a wringer washer. A short distance on, clothes hung straight and well pinned to a tight clothesline.

Mrs. Underwood invited them in, all apologetic about a living room that didn't need apology, though money would have helped.

"We just came to talk about Buddy, Mrs. Underwood. We're sorry if this is an inconvenient time."

"Well, my husband's not here. He works on Saturdays. And Buddy's gone with him. He always does. I don't have anything to offer you. I do have coffee. Would you like some coffee? And do sit down. The place is a mess."

Her wiry nervousness filled the room even when she was in the kitchen.

"We shouldn't have piled in on her like this," Mr. Berman said under his breath. He was seated in a small rocker. He hadn't removed his coat, and he held his hat on his left knee. Lila and Phil sat on a low sofa. Lila traced the pattern of a doily on the worn arm.

"No television," Phil whispered. "That's something."

Buddy's sister emerged from the back of the house, nodded shyly, and stood in the doorway to the living room.

Through the window, the afternoon sky was gray, no clouds, no branches of trees, but it seemed windy out there to the three of them, windy and brisk.

Mrs. Underwood carried a tray from the kitchen. "Buddy's done something," she said toward her daughter. "You know anything about this?"

The girl shook her head slowly and faded backward a little.

"He hasn't done anything," Mr. Berman said. "Not really. We're just concerned about some of his behavior."

She had put a plastic tray on the coffee table and removed the lid from the sugar bowl. "You go on out-

84

side," she said to her daughter. "You can get the clothes in."

The girl hesitated on her way through the living room and then walked quickly through the kitchen.

"What's he doing?" Mrs. Underwood rubbed her right palm against her hip bone, just below her waist. She didn't look at them.

"Well," Mr. Berman said.

"He touches himself," Lila said. "He fondles his private parts during school."

"We've spoken with him about this," Phil said. "We've sent him home."

Mrs. Underwood was nodding toward the floor. "You'll have to talk to my husband."

"We've written you. We've asked you to come in. You did get the letters?"

She continued to keep her head bowed, her face not visible. "You'll have to talk to my husband about it."

"We would like to. We think Billy needs counseling. The school doesn't have a counselor, but we could refer you."

"My husband works on Saturdays. All week and Saturdays, too."

"How can we talk with him then?"

"You could go there, I guess. Just behind the school. Phelp's Garage." She disappeared into the kitchen, and the daughter saw them to the door. The girl stood outside, and the wind whipped against her. She was slight, but well shaped, with rounded breasts and full thighs.

"Wonder what she thinks about all this," Phil said, but didn't press when Lila made no answer.

At the garage, Lila walked up and down the sidewalk while the three men talked. They had moved away from the work area, but the other workers and the waiting clients occasionally glanced toward the men, and wondered what was going on. Obviously, Chester Underwood's kid was in trouble. Billy himself was helping a mechanic lift a radiator from a car. Outside, the strong wind twisted the flag above the garage. Its shadow changed shapes and jerked across the cement. Lila fastened a scarf around her hair, and one man watched her. From a radio somewhere in the shop, a country blues sounded, the lyrics and melody garbled but long lasting.

"He don't cause no trouble, though?" Mr. Underwood said.

"No. But we can't let this continue."

"He ain't hurting anybody, right?"

"No. But you have to get him in counseling or control him someway."

Mr. Underwood wasn't sure what they meant by counseling, and when they explained, he explained, too, that he couldn't afford it. "My wife's sick, or she'd be working at the factory."

"You can get help through the county."

"Don't want it." They could tell he wanted that fact to sink in, wanted his pride to register as an important part of this conversation. The Underwoods did not take from the county. He motioned toward the garage. "I'm getting more work here. We'll be okay."

"We can't let Buddy in school until we know this is being dealt with. We have to think of the other students. And the teachers."

Mr. Underwood looked at Buddy. Buddy didn't giggle, but he didn't seem concerned, either. His mouth was partly open, and his gaze just floated past his father and back.

"I'll see he stops it." Mr. Underwood seemed through with the conversation, though he waited patiently.

They worried then that he would hurt the boy. Mr. Underwood wasn't a big man, and he didn't appear mean. He was much like Buddy, actually, though with a sharp, clear voice.

"Punishing him probably isn't a good idea," Phil said. "We wouldn't want you to misinterpret what we're saying."

"I don't whip my kids. I said he'll stop it. But I think you're making a problem up. That's what I think."

They left then, and conjectured about whether or not Buddy would be whipped.

"I don't think he'd hurt Buddy," Phil said, "but you can't tell about people."

"His wife was a sweet woman," Lila said.

"Well," Mr. Berman said. "We did what we had to do. I thank you both for coming along with me."

Mr. Berman spent the afternoon wondering if something like this should go to the school board, and mentally drafting phrases he could use if he had to. Finally he called one of his friends on the board, a man who owned a big farming operation and bought a new car every year, and they talked it over. That man discussed it with his wife.

Phil graded papers and watched a basketball game. Late in the afternoon he called Lila and asked if she wanted to drive down to Dexter and catch a movie. They had barbecue at the Pit and talked about job openings at the Cape. They weren't much attracted to one another, but in a town like Buxton, they took comfort in a familiar presence.

"Why didn't we drop it?" Lila said.

"Too late now."

"Maybe it's stress," Lila said. "It could be, couldn't it?"

"I guess. Some form of control."

Monday morning, Buddy sat down in study hall. Mrs. Hawkins just went about her business, deleting cards from the old system.

The school board held a closed session. They enjoyed the conversation. They drank coffee, and the men smoked, dropped ashes in a metal ashtray.

"This is off the record," they told Mr. Berman's secretary. "Don't put it in the report. Put something like, 'The Board discussed current discipline problems at the high school.'"

The secretary did as they asked, just substituting "difficulties" for "problems."

"And add that we're considering hiring a counselor."

"We don't have money for a counselor."

"The state would subsidize it."

"If we can get money for anything, let's get a new wing."

"Maybe a nurse. Serve in two functions, nurse and counselor."

"We need a science teacher more than a nurse."

"Air conditioning."

"Lyle Cochran handles science well enough."

They let the matter go, deciding it wasn't a discipline problem at all, and maybe the Underwoods' minister should be contacted. The Underwoods, though, didn't go to church, as far as anyone knew. One man was going to check on that, but he didn't. He was also a union representative for the factory, and became embroiled in some meetings about exhaust fans for the presser rooms.

Buddy Underwood came to school as always. Sometimes he'd open his book and read as the others did, sometimes work a problem or two. His left hand stayed in his pocket, but no one sent him from the classroom. During lunch hour, he sometimes shot baskets on the court. He didn't dress out, just removed his shoes and played in his street clothes and socks. He never attempted to join anyone else on the court during this free time, and no one joined him. Girls could look directly at him then. The second floor was a balcony floor, opening over the gym, and the girls would congregate there. They would eat candy bars, drink pop, and watch whoever was showing off that day. When it was Buddy, they sometimes said, "He's sickening, isn't he?" or, "He makes me sick." But they didn't sound disgusted or harsh. They could have been talking about a teacher or a parent. Sometimes they watched him in silence. A few times they applauded when he sank a basket. Their clapping sounded very loud and echoed, and the gym always seemed big and hollow then. Once when they applauded, Buddy smiled and bowed. That disconcerted them, and they stayed away for awhile.

In January, one of the rougher boys, Jewel Benson, got bored, dissatisfied living with no car, in a town with no movie theater or bowling alley or anything, and he got two of his friends to help him waylay Buddy. They drove in one friend's truck right behind Buddy and his sister, catcalling names they'd heard in Dexter and other places.

"Stop the truck," Jewel said. "Let's get him."

Jewel intended that he and one friend just pick Buddy up and toss him into the back of the truck, but they couldn't lift him, and no way could they drag him to it. He fought hard and nasty. His sister ran for help, but Buddy kicked and punched and cried. They hurt him, though. They kicked, too. He had a broken nose and broken collarbone. His father ran from the garage down the hill, with Buddy's sister trailing behind. By the time he arrived, someone had alerted Mr. Berman, and he was already there. Mr. Underwood shoved the principal away.

"Leave him alone. Leave my boy alone." He helped Buddy to his feet. Buddy's face was streaked with blood. They walked off together.

Mr. Berman started asking questions about who did it. The few kids who had seen it were quick to tell. They hung around school for awhile, too, hoping they'd see the next stage of the story. They didn't, though. Jewel wasn't in school the next day. They had to conjecture and try to find the rumor line.

Buddy missed one day of school. When he returned, his left arm was in a sling, and he had a clean, wide patch of gauze taped across his nose and another one over his left brow.

Larry Becraft walked down Buddy's aisle, though his own seat was two rows over, and said, "How you doing,

Buddy?" as he passed. Miles Barter nodded at Buddy when he entered the room. When Phil Weber announced a quiz and said, "Take out paper and pen," Kay Miller ripped a page from her notebook and leaned over to place it on Buddy's desk. She added a pencil a moment later. He giggled, and Kay wished he hadn't. When the quiz started, he slipped his left hand into his pocket, which made Kay regret doing anything at all, until, after class, Larry Becraft said, "That was a nice gesture, Kay." She was pleased, then, in a way that would last for most of her life.

All the teachers gave him passing grades that year. It was a hot, sultry spring, the teachers' lounge had only one window, and though Buddy hadn't scored well on the state mastery exams, he hadn't scored as low as some kids with a lot more going for them.

"Besides," Lila Murphy said, "he certainly gets full credit for attendance."

Everyone laughed.

"Some kids you hope will get the flu," someone said.

"And some ask to be failed."

"Not Buddy, though. That's not the real problem."

"No."

He was, they decided, probably at least as smart as his sister, and she was a better-than-average student.

When he returned in the fall, teachers and students thought Buddy might have changed. He was slimmer, for one thing, and his jaw and mouth had firmed up. He could even meet someone's eyes for a second or two. But he preferred his pocket.

Three more years Buddy attended school faithfully,

sporadically worked as requested, and consistently took exams. The family must have fared better. Buddy and his sister occasionally had new clothes. When the girl performed with the school chorus at the Christmas show, the Underwoods attended. Rows of folding chairs filled the gym floor, and the Underwoods sat near the front. Chester Underwood wore a hat, but took it off the minute he sat down. Most people didn't know who they were until they saw Buddy next to them. Those who did recognize them believed they were a normal-looking family. Mrs. Underwood was wearing a man's overcoat, but many farm wives did that—men's clothing cost less. After the performance, the Underwoods even stood in the anteroom long enough for Mr. Berman to approach them and shake Mr. Underwood's hand. Phil Weber and Lila Murphy each said, "Hi, Buddy," and stated to Mrs. Underwood that the chorus was exceptionally good this year.

"You don't sing, Buddy?" Phil asked, and Buddy shook his head.

"At least," Phil later said to Lila, "he didn't giggle."

The giggling stopped. In fact, Buddy's mouth closed. He began to stare out the window instead of at the blackboard. His dark floating irises would reflect the hazy light, and sometimes girls thought he was really quite good-looking, sort of sad looking, with such beautiful eyes. He thinned more and more, and his shoulders thus seemed broader. Some of them were pleased that he looked up from the basketball court. Kay Miller even wore a slip with lace edging the bottom. Her girlfriend wore a blouse with a scooped neck and leaned with her elbows on the balcony.

"You flirting with Buddy Underwood?" Kay asked and teased her friend for a day or two. In the teachers' lounge, the progress of Buddy's family was noted as if he were one of their honor students. "Buddy's mother is apparently working at the factory." "The Underwoods have moved into town. They bought the old Wright place." "Is Buddy's dad any good with transmissions?"

The year after Buddy and his sister graduated, Buddy's name appeared among many others who had recently enlisted during the recruiting at Dexter. Phil Weber was leaving Buxton that year, and he recalled Buddy Underwood as one of his better experiences in small-town America. "The persistence of the individual," he said to Lila, "who will, by damn, prevail." Lila, too, was leaving, but only for the Cape school district, where facilities were better, and where parents didn't work just down the street. They packed during the peaceful days after school was dismissed, when the trees were flush and the humid air smelled of many flowers. They met for one last dinner together and said they'd keep in touch.

They had been gone over a year when a picture of Buddy, in uniform, appeared on the front page of the weekly newspaper. The heading, "Local Man Hero," drew Mr. Berman's ardent attention, but then his eyes caught the word "fallen" a couple of lines down. He folded the paper immediately, carrying it and a cup of coffee to his backyard. He sat in a lawn chair from which he could see the narrow main street leading up, splitting just at the steeper rise to the courthouse. He sipped his coffee and eventually, already grieving for small-town boys and boys all over the world, opened the newspaper.

Buddy hadn't died.

Though Mr. Berman was a restrained man, pride flushed him, maybe even a tinge of joy. Buddy, or William John Allan Dale Underwood, had braved enemy fire to defend and rescue a fallen comrade. Mr. Berman read the article again. His lips moved with each word. He felt kinship with this boy, this kid who defied all predictions, all concerns. This was what it meant to be human. This was the very gut of education and civilization. Patience. Mr. Berman strode into his house, rummaged noisily for scissors, and then cut the article out neatly. He clipped, too, the masthead, *Green County News,* and placed both items inside the big Bible his wife kept on the coffee table—a family Bible, she called it, though they had never had children.

Later, Mr. Berman acquired more copies of the article. Two of them he mailed to Lila Murphy. "You can send the extra to Phil Weber," he wrote, "if you know where he's teaching." Lila didn't know, but she kept both articles because she couldn't throw such news into the trash, could she? It would be sacrilege, or a slap in the face of fate, or something like that.

Other people read the article, too, and some saved it. One old veteran, still limping from a war in his youth, carefully and squarely tacked the article to the bulletin board at the post office. "By God," he said, "if we can put the country's most wanted there, we can put its most best." He laughed at his wit and way with words. Small-town people weren't stupid, just freer. Almost everyone remembered Buddy Underwood. Sure, they did. And always would, too. Now he had fought for them, risked his life on foreign soil, defending everyone in the world. They were subtly and genuinely very fond of him, of the whole family. Those Underwoods were good, solid people, long-time residents of Buxton.

# ⸙ Blue Baby ⸙

My brother is big, deep voiced, dark eyed, and more than fills the living room with his presence, fills the house, actually, so I know where he is every moment, know the signs that mean he will leave, not abruptly, never that, but surely and steadily, kissing each of us first with a soft "Bye, Sis," "Bye, Sis," "Bye, Mom," and then away to his own life.

So when he goes in the kitchen for one more piece of pie, I trail him down the hall, stand in his shadow cast not by light—the kitchen window is on the other side of the room—but by his being my brother who is six years younger than I and who has turned forty, with white streaks in the thick shock of black hair, hands larger than my grandfather's were, and a look in his eyes so gentle I want to be in their sight. I knew him when he was forming. I knew him when he came home from the hospital, a "blue baby," Mother said. "We have to give him special care." I bathed him, loved him, kissed his sweet sleeping eyes.

"When you finish," I say, "will you walk with me in the backyard?"

96

"Sure, Sis. For a little while, anyhow."

He has a pretty smile, the outline of his mouth sharply etched, and when he smiles, just before, immediately before, the corners of his mouth turn up and a dimple appears on either side.

Down the hall from the kitchen is the room that was his. It sits lower than the rest of the house, with a step down that has a false top. There he hid his share of the bottled sodas Mother brought home, his share of the bananas, and probably other things. To that room he fled when relatives came, carrying his plate of country food, each portion set apart by the bread-crust divider he carefully fashioned.

"They're not *my* relatives," he would say.

My sister, Ruth, and I share the same father—our mother married him twice. James's father came in between and was gone before James was born.

He comes out the back door and down the steps heavily, but he's an agile man. Not all survivors are as strong as he is. He smiles at me. "How you doing, Sis?"

I love his voice. I wish I could express the sound.

"Fine." He lets me take his hand, and we walk past the old storage shed, the hen house, both now filled with discarded furniture from all our lives.

"Remember the chickens?" I ask.

"Sure. Not these, but chickens, yes. I hate them. They're sort of burned in my memory."

"That's right. You worked at a chicken plant, sometime after I left."

"My junior year. Five mornings a week. Got up at four o'clock, worked from five to seven, got to school by eight thirty."

"I'm sorry."

"I stank. All the livelong day. They're filthy creatures." He says this matter-of-factly, like a street address
he happens to remember.

The backyard slopes, hollyhock here, apple tree
there, honeysuckle meshing white and green over the
cellar mound. Here he practiced shooting his rifle,
breaking the town code which Mother ignored and
insisted that I did, too. He was nine then, and a bullet
ricocheted from something and shot back to clip his ear-
lobe. Mother still allowed him to shoot. I'd kiss that ear-
lobe this minute if he were a smaller man.

"I wish you approved of me," I tell him, keeping my
voice casual, strolling on toward the ditch.

He squeezes my hand. "I'm proud of you. You've
done a hell of a lot."

"But I know you think I should have stayed married."

"I liked your husband. He seemed like an all right guy."

"I wasn't happy."

He shrugs, lets go of my hand, scoops up half-rotted
apples and throws them toward the ditch.

When James was twelve, and my father more often
drunk than sober, James would sit in his room holding
the rifle across his legs. Once I went in there to tell him
to put it away, and he said, "No. If he hits her, I'll kill
him." That was the year I married and left Buxton. He
may have held that rifle every night for six more years. I
never asked.

Mother says she pays my nephew, James's son, to mow
her yard, but I can't mention that, that he shouldn't
charge her. Surely James owes her some kind of son's
duty.

The garden is dried, vines now stobs, leaves sun-burned brittle. Our mother used to can after work and on weekends. When James was a young boy, he would take a backpack with skillet, flour, and a small jar of lard, his fishing pole over his shoulder, and walk out to the Castor River. He always said he caught something, cooked and ate it before coming home. He never ate dinner those Saturday nights. I don't know if he was catching fish or building pride. Once when he went fishing on a Saturday, some bigger boys teased him. They broke his fishing pole. I know because I was sitting at the kitchen table when he came home. He trudged down the hall, all brown and frowning, head down, passed me, and stopped by Mother's side.

"They broke my pole," he said.

"Who did?"

"Clyde Welker and some other guys."

She soothed him. I remember her drying her hands and squatting down by him. He was maybe eight. He slapped away her touch.

"It was the only thing I had," he said.

I remember thinking that was true, though I didn't know why. Unbearably true.

"Do you hold anything against me?" I ask. "From when you were little? I had to take care of you, you know. I had to play the mother."

"No," he says. "I don't remember much of that."

He has squatted down by the edge of the ditch. I stand next to him, rest my hand on his thick hair, and he doesn't pull away.

"Remember running at me with the clothesline pole?"

"You squirted water on me," he says.

"Yes, I did. But that couldn't have caused such anger. You were so mad you were purple."

"I was mad a lot. Still am."

James is a good father, Mother says. He dotes on his children. He works overtime, even on weekends, and gives them whatever they want. They adore him, as they should.

But he struck his wife, or so Ruth told me. Ruth thinks it happened only once. Mother talked to him about it, and he said, "She pushed me too far. I can only take so much."

Mother and Ruth have come outside. They sit in the lawn chairs near the cellar mound. "Don't be sociable," Ruth calls. "That's all right. Just go off by yourselves."

"I feel like I let you down," I say. "I want us to be close, and I don't know how to do it."

"I love you, Sis. We're as close as we could be after living apart all these years."

"No. Something's missing."

"No, there's not." He stands up and hugs me and kisses my cheek. We walk back toward the others, and I know he's leaving soon. He sits and listens to Mother talk about the neighbor encroaching on her property line, listens to Ruth describe her daughter's singing voice. James doesn't talk much.

When he was in basic training, he called Mother to get him out, to find some way to spare him this bad choice. She refused, explaining that he might hate her in later life.

When he was in Vietnam, I wrote him, but not often. I always meant to send him packages of cookies, pictures, magazines. But I was pregnant and working and unhappy. Later always seemed a better time.

Mother says he writes letters to presidents, to congressmen, to VA hospitals, and has done so for years. She says sometimes they're crazy letters, angry letters. He has high blood pressure. He stayed in Vietnam longer than he had to. He wouldn't come home.

I ironed his baby clothes. I held him while Mother worked. I remember how his jeans were always too big for his little frame, and the belt always too long, the tip drooping down. I remember him about four, curled in a print chair somewhere, the collar of his plaid shirt gaping and his small collarbones like wings, his eyes fluttering with uneasy sleep. I've heard that when he first came home from Vietnam, he kept the radio as loud as it would go. He only told Mother one story, something about finally getting to bathe and standing naked while death dropped all around him rather than get dirty one more time.

We trail him up the yard and to his truck.

"Well, Sis," he says. "Good to see you. Take care."

He kisses each of us, as is his way, and hugs me once again. I'd like to rest there awhile, against that strong-beating heart, but I don't dare. He wouldn't let me, and I understand.

# ⊰A Near-Perfect Gift⊱

As soon as Dellie and Janey drove away, Oida carefully stepped down from her front porch and walked around the side of the house. She was a small red-haired woman, humped from years of labor in a sewing factory, but even at seventy still dressed and moved daintily. Now, though, she was angry, and her hands trembled as she pulled dead petals from her flowers. "Love me, my foot," she muttered to the rosebush. "They don't want to miss my dying." She retied the stake string higher so the straggly rose branches cleared the ground. "I shouldn't have planted you here. You need more sun. Try anyhow. I haven't got the strength to transplant you." Still agitated, she watered the plants, then dragged the hose to the backyard. If she stayed busy long enough, she'd calm down. She didn't understand her sisters. Half-sisters, really. They were as foreign to her as if they'd had a different father, too, not just a different mother. "Cold women," she said. "They don't fool me." She filled the green birdbath, letting the water swirl up, foam, and cascade over the side. Occasionally she sprayed a thin stream upward to make a tiny rainbow just feet away. She liked that.

Oida had placed the hose on its roller and was removing a floating leaf from the birdbath, when a patch of lawn caught her attention. It had moved. She studied it a moment, then put her hands behind her back and walked toward the patch. She waited in the long shadow of her house. The spot moved again, and her breath quickened a little. She didn't think it was a mole down there, though it could be. They came and went each summer, sometimes rumpling her ground, sometimes the neighbors'. She never killed them because they were impatient, migratory creatures, and would move on before she could kill them anyway. Most people didn't seem to know that—Janey, for instance—and wasted energy and anger tracking a gone thing, then bragged that they must've killed it, because the tunnels stopped. A sharp-eyed person would see the tunnels beginning anew just a house or two down.

No. It wasn't a mole. The earth was being pushed up, cracking, though still webbed by grass. Something was on its way up and out. Oida quickly glanced around her as if she might find a person to come look at this, at this whatever-it-was. She thought, *Snake, lizard,* but she believed, without any real clue why, that it wasn't anything she'd ever seen coming out of the earth before.

"Oh!" she said, as tiny claws inched through the aperture, gripped, and tugged. Hairless, folded wings emerged, shielding a pointed, small, rattish face. For one flash of a second, Oida thought, *Demon!* and her heart clutched. But then she knew just what it was—a bat.

A bat, but still a wonder, crawling up out of the ground like that.

"My Lord." She bent down to watch it slowly emerge. "What were you doing down there?"

It hissed at her, and fear supplanted wonder. Oida scurried to the shed and came back quickly, using the shovel like a cane. The bat was watching her. It even jumped toward her twice, as if it could ward her off.

"I don't like killing anything," Oida said, "but you could be rabid. Probably are." She raised the shovel, and the late sun cast her elongated, armed shadow over the bat. It flopped onto its back. The wings stretched out like gray silk fans, and there, lying against the delicate membranes but clutching the bat's skinny body, were two babies.

Oida lowered the shovel. "Smart little thing, aren't you? Had to show me what you were fighting for."

Now she didn't know what to do. The neighbors' yards were empty. Her voice wasn't strong enough to yell for anyone. A high whistling whine was the loudest sound she could make, and no one was likely to come running for that.

"I could just go inside," she said, "but then a cat might get you. And besides, I wouldn't know where you were. I wouldn't want you surprising me again."

It still lay in that female-plea position.

Oida gave up. She could never strike it, or let anyone else do so. "I'm not going to hurt you." With both hands, and very slowly, she pushed the shovel blade forward. "I'm going to scoop you up now, so don't panic or anything. I'm going to scoop you up and carry you and your babies to the ditch."

The bat didn't move, didn't even hiss. Its black pellet eyes were cold, though. "You know, don't you?" Oida lifted the now-laden shovel. "You know when to fight and when not to. Good girl."

Her yard was a long downward grade to the drainage ditch. Even so, she found walking and balancing the shovel difficult. She was lightheaded from the heat, and, she supposed, from the excitement. "You better not be the death of me," she whispered. She studied the options. Trees in various stages of decay lined the upper rim. Below were bare roots, rotting branches, and tangles of vines and weeds. A little jungle. Bats belonged in trees, but Oida couldn't very well manage that. She couldn't raise her arms above her head at all. If she left the bat on the ground, it might manage to get up the tree, but maybe it couldn't fly with babies hanging on. Oida didn't know. She didn't want to leave it for some other creature's food. She laid the shovel down so the handle jutted over the edge, muttered, "You stay put," and grasped a sturdy root to lower herself a foot or so. When her feet were firmly planted, she grabbed the wooden handle, pulled the shovel over and down, and shook the threesome into the dark recess behind exposed roots.

"This is it," she said. "You can hide, or you can climb the tree. There's food all around you, and water just feet away. Best I can do."

Oida had to rest twice on the way to the house. Then she had to put the shovel away. She wanted very much to be able to run back down the yard and look once again at that mother bat, but she couldn't do it. She couldn't run even to save her own life. Old people had to settle for what was possible, whether it be pleasure or pain. This new story of hers, though, was definitely a pleasure. She loved things like this. She wanted to look up bats and find out what one might be doing down in the ground, but she didn't have an encyclopedia. She wanted to call everybody she knew. She latched the screen door behind her, bolted the main back door, then went to the bathroom, so later she wouldn't have to interrupt her phone calls. In the kitchen, she looked out the window while water heated for coffee. The light was already dimmer, and the ditch trees turning darker. Such color changes always amazed her—how trees were blacker than night, actually, when one knew they weren't really black at all; how the moon was ghost white in the daytime, yellow and orange and red at night; how some flowers turned violent red when they didn't get any sun. How could a person ever know the real nature of a thing when it changed all the time? The world was a magic wonder, that was for certain.

Halfway down the hall with her coffee, Oida remembered that she hadn't entered the bat on her calendar. She returned to the kitchen and wrote the time, followed by "Bat came out of the ground." She saved her calendars. If the same strange thing happened twice, she'd know. She thought maybe her record of patterns, odd little workings of the Lord, might make a good book in the right hands. Not hers, of course. She wasn't educated. She wasn't stupid, though. Too cowardly, maybe, but not stupid.

With the phone base cradled in her lap, Oida called her son. She felt like the bearer of good news, and wanted the chance to set up the tale, step by step, how she had been inside all day because of the heat, but had ventured out to get rid of Dellie and Janey and to fill the birdbath, how the air was stifling and made her weak, how a few blades of grass had trembled in the late sun and made her pause. She wanted to describe the backyard at that moment, washed in dimming sunlight with huge shadows just beginning to fade into the earth, the silence of coming evening, the absence of sound, the appearance of those tiny claws and that miniature devil face.

But her son rushed her. He didn't tell her to hurry up or say he had guests or work or had just arrived home or was just leaving. But he wasn't *in* the story with her. He chuckled and offered little clues of his attention. "Uh huh. It was pretty damned hot out today, okay." "Maybe you should get out more often. The heat wouldn't make you weak." "Oh, a mole." "Not a mole? What then?" "You sure about that? That's something, isn't it?" He had the sweetest, honey-soft voice, and she always felt loved when he spoke to her, like he was leaning down to put his arms around her. But he butchered her story. She had to tell it in little whisper gasps. She wanted him to be in awe, like she was. He called to his wife, "Hey, Franny, Mom saw a bat crawl out of the ground. Yeah," and then came back with, "Go on, Mom. What'd you do with the thing?" She wanted first to build the drama of the underwing babies, to get in the breathlessness of the sight, but she was somehow forced to jump ahead and tell of the disposal at the tree root. "I'll be damned," he said, and relayed that information, too, to his wife.

"She had babies," Oida added, far too late.

"Right then? When you dropped her at the tree?"

"No. Not then!" Oida backtracked and explained how the mother bat had plopped over, but she couldn't get any enthusiasm or energy now. She was suddenly weary of talking against the strength of his interest and still-youth at forty-two, and the presence of his wife taking up threads of the conversation when Oida was the spinner. She forgave him, though. He worked two jobs to support his family. And when he had come home from that crazy jungle war, he had been unable to speak a complete sentence for almost three months. He had just smiled a lot. It was a God-crazy smile that broke her heart.

Oida prepared before calling her youngest daughter. She thought through the event step by step, and verbalized it to herself. She changed some of her wording to fit it better, and even paused where she'd want to pause. This child of hers was also fond of creatures and odd things. She read God's hand into every event, though Oida wasn't sure she had instilled or even encouraged such an attitude in her children. Oida believed in God, and Jesus, and she believed all the universe down to her own veins was his glorious handiwork, but she didn't sing hallelujah or cry at every manifestation. She would've been dead long ago if she had done so. And she believed her youngest daughter, thirty-nine, might not live to see sixty if she didn't tone down her reactions to normal life. She was always breaking out in hives, or having to take tranquilizers.

The daughter listened calmly at first, just punctuating the tale with "Uh huh, uh hum," until Oida reached the trembling ground. Then all vocal responses stopped while Oida told about the tiny, tiny bare-naked fragile things clinging to the underside of their momma. "Oh my Lord," her daughter whispered. "I can't imagine . . . babies. And she was showing you. She knew what she was doing, didn't she, Momma?" The hush of her voice was just right, but she took off into her frenzied talk. "Did you get a picture of it, Momma? You think it might still be there in the morning? How big's the hole? You can take a picture of the hole it came out of. That'll prove it. I feel like driving down there right this minute."

"It's too dark to see anything now, honey."

"I know. I'm not coming. I just want to. I never saw anything like that. I wish I had. Maybe it'll happen again. What are you going to do?"

"About what?"

"About that hole. The bat. You think it'll still be there in the morning?"

"I know the hole will, unless I'm a crazy woman. I don't know about the bat. She already goes places I don't think bats go. No telling what she'll do."

The daughter laughed, and Oida did, too. Laughing was good, and she enjoyed it, but it wasn't what she intended and it wasn't what she wanted. She hung up and rethought her encounter, to bring it back. She was already losing it, and she had one more child to call. And two sisters, if she wanted. Dellie and Janey. She didn't want to think about them. "If you fall or something one day," Janey had said, "you'll be glad we keep an eye on you."

Now Oida knew how she should have responded. "Keeping an eye on somebody might *make* 'em fall." She glanced at the wall clock. She had tacked its cord along the edge of the window, but she hadn't been able to hide the ugly strip from the base to the sill. Nothing was ever just exactly perfect. Except maybe sleep. Oida thought sleep was maybe a near-perfect thing. She liked dreaming. Answers floated around, and you could sort them out with a little thinking.

She put the phone aside, stood to turn on the television. She never watched news at night, because sleeping with the ills of the world in your mind wasn't healthy. She flicked channels till one showed a group of monkeys chittering wildly at a snake slithering down a skinny branch and roping onto the ground. The snake was yellow liquid. And evil. The bat hadn't *really* looked evil. More tortured than anything. She turned down the volume and returned to the phone.

The oldest daughter was a professor in a university four hundred miles north. She was a hard-working, worn-down woman, who had loved too many men too much and had come into her education and job late. She wasn't a patient person. Not at all. Once she had screamed at Oida, "I've got to get out of here before you drive me as crazy as you are." Oida had never forgotten the exact words, tone, or situation. The scene sometimes popped up in her mind and played itself over and over and ruined entire days. But Oida loved that girl, just like she loved her other children. She'd give them a better nature if she could. She'd hand them hope and happiness like a gift if it were possible. But it wasn't. Life was work and pain and little moments of joy like a blink in eternity. That's how God had set it up. It wasn't the best way, looking at it from this side, but no telling what it looked like from his view. Anyhow, he did it, and he got to call the shots. Fair had nothing to do with it. She had told her children that.

The oldest daughter listened quietly. Oida could hear the intake of breath which meant her daughter was smoking a cigarette. She smoked maybe fifty or sixty of them a day. When she visited Oida, she went out on the porch every fifteen minutes or so, even in the coldest weather. Oida had bought a smoke filter and put it in the bathroom one winter, but after her daughter was gone, she'd had to wash every towel in the cupboard and it seemed to her that even the wallpaper had soaked up the tobacco scent. And her own throat was raspy.

"And so," Oida ended, with her voice nearly gone from so much talking, "I pulled the shovel to me while I held onto a root with one hand. I had to grip the shovel down by the blade, you know, so I wouldn't spill the little things out, and maybe they'd fall into the water. The shovel was heavy, but I sort of swung it to me, and she lay just as still and steady, like she was helping me as best she could. I nudged the shovel blade up to the root cavity and shook it just the littlest bit, and the minute she felt that dirt and dark around her, she scrambled back out of sight. She trusted me till she didn't have to anymore. I know what she was thinking. I would've been the same way in the same situation."

"I love that story, Momma. It gives me chills."

*That* was the right response.

"I know. Me, too."

"I don't think I could've handled it."

"Sure you could have. There wasn't nothing to handle."

"Scares me a little."

"What's scary about it? A little momma bat, that's all."

"You know that's not all."

"No. But it's no big thing. No worry thing, for sure."

"Think about it. A bat coming out of the ground. Knowing enough to flop on its back."

"I did think about it. That's why I called you." This child had always been spooky, scared of the dark, scared of God. "What if he's not a good god?" she had once said. "What if he's a mean-hearted bastard?" She had become an atheist rather than admit he might be up there watching her all the time. Oida didn't want to get her started again. "If I'd known it was going to scare you, honey, I wouldn't have called. You don't need any more worries."

"No, I like hearing it. I'm going to call a friend of mine in the science department, see if he's heard of anything like this. I know bats live in trees and caves, but I'd like to know if they ever just claw up out of the dirt."

Oida felt a chill of a different sort, and she didn't want to be frightened near bedtime. "Oh, don't bother anyone with this. It's not that special. You tell me how you been doing. Is your blood pressure down?"

Oida watched the television screen while her daughter talked, just to keep the room from seeming so suddenly dark and dingy. The show had changed. Some man was creeping up to the side of a house. The shadow of a woman moved behind a curtain, and he watched. Oida flicked the control to another channel.

"Maybe," she said into the phone, "you should give up that job and move nearer to me. Or near your girls.

That would be even better. You're just lonely, honey. That's all that's wrong with you. You wouldn't need that blood pressure medication if you could be near your kids." She carried the phone with her while she turned on the other two lamps.

When she hung up, she felt soaked with her daughter's fearful nature. Life was so wearying, such a struggle.

Oida slept in the front bedroom, which she rarely did. She usually preferred one of the two hallway bedrooms. They were tiny, but seemed more sheltered. Each was wallpapered, had a nice throw rug by the bed, a reading lamp, and some magazines. She wanted more space tonight, though, and wanted to be near the front door. She didn't know why exactly, but the feeling was good enough. Instinct was instinct. She felt like she might need to fly off somewhere, and she didn't want to be trapped.

She lay on her side and tried to recapture the earlier evening in her backyard. She couldn't. She had to fight to dispel the heavy black of the bedroom with dark curtains and no windows open, the oppressive closeness of a shut room. Finally, she got out of bed and raised a window a few inches. The night did have noise, even when it wasn't a particular sound. But she knew when she was hearing it. A rustling of life or of settling down. Maybe the rustle of the whole world. It was a pleasant sound, very soothing, everyone together at last. She got back in bed and closed her eyes. She almost had the whole backyard scene again when she felt herself falling asleep. She thought one of God's real gifts was sleep. She had always welcomed it like the gift it was.

When Oida woke next morning, she was terribly sad, and she knew she had dreamed something painful or disturbing. She opened her kitchen curtains, and at the sight of the backyard, she recalled yesterday evening and felt a quick interest in having her coffee, getting dressed, and going outside. She sat at the table side nearest the stove, from where she could see the ditch. The phone rang, and she knew it was Dellie. She thought about not answering. If Dellie and Janey wanted to worry, let them worry. But she couldn't do it. She had never refused human contact in her life. What you did to others would get done to you.

She didn't intend to tell Dellie about the bat, but it just slipped out. "You'll never guess what I saw yesterday. A bat crawled from a hole in my backyard. It had babies under its wing. I don't know how it got under there or what drove it out, but it was absolutely the most surprising thing I've seen in a long time."

"You sure it was a bat, Oida?"

And then she hated herself for selling out her story in return for a morning phone call from a stone-cold sister.

"I know a bat when I see one." She hung up on Dellie and was glad she did.

Then she showered as hurriedly as she could without risking a fall. She never looked at herself in the mirror anymore when she combed her hair or brushed her teeth. Who could like seeing what old age did to them, especially in the morning? She just opened the medicine cabinet and swung the mirror out of the way. Later in the day, when her body had warmed up to movement, she'd check herself out. And she never went to town or

anywhere without a bit of Tangee lipstick and face powder. Now she donned heavy blue slacks with an elastic
waistband, so she could bend comfortably, a long-
sleeved white shirt, and white socks and tennis shoes.
She might have to get down in that ditch to see.

The morning sun made prisms of light over the trees.
The grass held dew, and wet blades clung to her tennis
shoes. The edges of the rubber soles were turning green.
She loved this. The way everything changed in a minute.
At the edge of the ditch, she said, "Well, you down
there?" Bending, she placed her right hand against the
tree, stepped down by digging her heels into the dirt,
and squatted to look behind the twisted roots. Nothing.
The little things were gone. "Got away, didn't you?" She
glanced around the base of the tree and a few feet
beyond. Then she scanned the branches for a sight of
soft gray. Nothing. A blue jay screeched at her. They
were noisy creatures. They would be good in time of war
if birds could fight. That wasn't the nature of war. A
warrior was a warrior, though, bird or man. Little bat-
tles everywhere. Her son had served his time. He was a
warrior, too. Lots of people were. She liked it here, with
the sun dappling silver and shadow all around her, the
water below flowing shallow but fast enough to cleanse
itself. This morning could be anytime, when she was five
or ten or twenty or forty. But she was seventy, and she
didn't know when that had happened. No one ever knew
how old they were. It surprised them every day. And it
wasn't a pleasant surprise.

"Well, you're gone, and I'm glad." She started to
ascend, but her foot turned or just gave out. She stumbled, twisted around to avoid falling backward down the

slope, and couldn't check her forward movement. At the water's edge, her feet caught in the mire, and she careened toward flat limestone. She thrust out her arms, felt them scrape against the stone, then lay stunned. Her breath came in gasps. Her eyes couldn't make the world stand still; the shadows and light swirled wildly. She was afraid to move, so she didn't, not for a long while. The water just barely covered the stone, brushed against her left cheek. The blue jay screeched at her again. At least, she hoped it was the same one. She liked him. She wanted him to stay around so she wouldn't die. If something alive was yelling at her, she wouldn't die. She closed her eyes, but that was worse. Red dots popped up like eyes. "You're not dead, old girl," she whispered. She pushed herself up very slowly. Water swirled over her legs and around her, caught a strain of red from her left wrist. She had cut herself, deep and jagged. When she lifted her arm out of the water, the blood spurted, and she felt faint. She immersed it again. "You take hold of this, Oida," she said. Those were her father's words, when he had been a young man and she got frightened. "A person can handle anything," he had said many times. "You just got to take hold of it. If you die, you die. There are worse things than dying."

The limestone bothered her. Her own mother's headstone had been limestone, and it washed away during a flood one year. No one knew for sure where the grave was. And Oida could see what had cut her wrist. The bottom of a bottle. A beer bottle. That, too, seemed like a sign. Her husband had been an alcoholic, had abused the kids and her, and she hadn't been brave enough to stop him. She should have left him, but she waited all hopeful and loving till he abandoned her and the children. She felt like she was in her own dream, one she could almost understand and didn't want to. She shook it away. Maybe this was just God's way of telling her to be thankful she was alive at all. "Lord," she said, toward the patch of sky above the trees, "if this is a message from you, I can't decipher it."

When the blood slowed to a trickle, she stood up gingerly. There was nothing to grasp. She took very short, careful steps back to semi-solid ground, dropped to her knees, and crawled up the slope. She wasn't fool enough to fall twice. Only at the level did she stand, and then watched each step all the way to the house and into the kitchen. She took two aspirin and went in the bathroom to wash up. She cleaned the wound and wrapped gauze around her wrist. When she was putting on fresh clothes, just as she was buttoning the pink blouse, a flash of last night's dream came to her. She let the memory settle while she heated water for coffee and watched the sunlight spill across her yellow tiled floor.

"Something about a cave," she said toward the teakettle. She leaned against the counter. "A cave and God." She spooned coffee into her cup, poured the water, and watched the bubbles float to the side and gradually dissipate. Little dark ocean waves. She sat down. The table was metal, with a red checkered top. She liked bright things. If she'd been God, it would have been daylight all the time, rest or not. But that wasn't the dream. God and a cave and unhappiness and pain. Escape. Creatures screaming and running to the walls, not to the mountains, not to the caves, but from the caves, from the mountains, out to the open air.

"I dreamed of hell," she said. That scared her. She stood up. She couldn't sit at the table. She felt like closing the curtains against the rising sun. But that was stupid, because it was the dark she'd dreamed about. A dark cave hell. She glanced up at the bright glare still coming up over the world and was blinded for a moment, had to stare at her yard while colors swam and then fell back into shapes she recognized. She wasn't going to think about this. "Maybe I owe you for not breaking my neck at that ditch." She put the cup in the sink. Through the window, she saw her neighbor two doors down carrying out his trash. The human sight warmed her, though she didn't like the man personally. She closed her eyes and bowed her head. It was God she should be thinking of. "If I owe you for saving my life, you have my thanks. I mean it."

Then she went outside again. Everything had changed, like the world was filmy, muted. Nothing seemed real. She sat down at her picnic table. She could have died in the ditch. After all, she'd hung up on Dellie, and her kids were too far away or working all the time. She had had to crawl out, an ugly scramble for a short time of more living. Death was an ugly thing even in the best of circumstances. She remembered her father's death. Suffering so long. So long. Out of his head the last months. She and her sisters had driven to the rest home every Saturday. Dellie would say the prayers he didn't remember anymore, her voice booming with conviction. Janey would stand with her arms under her breasts, scowling like she disapproved of all this commotion. Janey couldn't look anything in the face. Never could. When she was little, her mother used to whip her with a willow switch, and Janey wouldn't even cry. She just stared off somewhere. But the day their father died, Dellie and Janey weren't there. Only Oida was. She had wakened knowing and had sped the fifty-some miles to the Poplar Bluff rest home. Blackbirds were all along the highway. Hordes of them. When they swooped up, the blood-red wingtips surprised and frightened her, but only momentarily. Everything was a sign. Everything in this world was connected. At the home, she sat on his bed and held his dear head against her breasts. The cold crept up his arms. She felt it in her hands, then her own arms. She had felt such guilt at welcoming his death. Something was dreadfully wrong when a woman had to long for the death of her father.

Now Oida stood up, got a sturdy stick from a pile near the ditch, looked around for her bat family, then walked back to the hole. She squatted and examined it. It was small, not quite as big as a half-dollar. She didn't know how the little thing had squeezed up and through it. She poked down gently, but the stick stopped at a few inches. She thought maybe the tunnel veered off. That bat hadn't materialized under the soil. It had come from somewhere. She sat down, not really weary. Another flash from her dream came to her, of creatures climbing up walls, frantic, finding ways out through the tinest chink, scurrying, ugly, hopeful, and brave little demons. "You come on out," she said toward the hole. "Anytime, day or night. Wherever you want. Dig up my yard all you need to." She stood, keeping her head bowed like she wasn't up to anything. It seemed to her the whole ground beneath her trembled, just for a second, and she trembled in return. "It is unbearable, I know." She walked down to toss the stick back in the pile, and headed toward her house. She felt simultaneously sad, good, and firmly resolved about something.

When her son came by, she let him search her backyard and scan the tree where she'd left the creatures. She held the cuff of her sleeve to hide the bandage.

"You shouldn't have let it go, Mom, though I understand. They breed pretty fast, you know. You sure you want them all over the place?"

"I imagine they're already here," she said. "Or where would that one have come from?"

He chuckled. She liked pleasant sounds, however brief they were. He could have died in the war. She was thankful for that gift, too. But it didn't change things.

Her youngest daughter came down on the weekend, and the oldest daughter called. They had both talked with everyone they could, and bats simply don't come up out of the ground. Not in the center of a yard. She had to have a cave somewhere on her property. Maybe coming from the ditch. Water erosion or something.

"That's probably it," Oida said. "I'm not worried about it."

They both wanted to have the property examined.

"No," Oida told both of them. "It's my place, and like I said, I'm not worried about it. And I don't want you kids to worry about it, either. You let me handle this. You got all you can do now." She didn't tell either of them about the fall, or the wound. When she cleaned her wrist, she felt very strong for keeping this secret.

Dellie and Janey came by on Sunday afternoon. Dellie didn't go in the backyard at all, but Janey did. Oida saw her standing with her arms across her midriff, looking at the broken ground. When she came inside, she said, "Looks to me like somebody just dug it up from this side."

"I didn't make it up," Oida said.

"I didn't say that."

"You said it every way but straightout."

"You gotta stop getting so mad at little things, Oida." Dellie placed her hand over Oida's.

Oida liked that. Dellie's hand was big, a most competent hand. But it was warm, too, and surprisingly soft underneath. She and Janey were Oida's baby sisters, and the harshness of their lives more than matched her own. Oida didn't know anyone who didn't struggle, who didn't have to fight some kind of misery almost every day. It scared her, thinking of where they all might be.

"Yes, I do," she said. She supposed she had surprised them both. "I'm tired of getting mad. You girls want some cake?"

"What'd you do to your arm?" Dellie turned Oida's hand slightly. "That's right on the wrist, isn't it?"

"Took a tiny fall, but nothing to worry anybody about. I caught myself just fine."

Dellie took Oida's other hand and turned it over.

"I'm no fool, Dellie," Oida said, "and no liar, either."

"Nobody said you were. Don't get upset."

Janey ate her cake while peering out the window. Oida remembered how angry and hard their mother had been. But then, she had been the second wife. She had had a lovely voice, though, and sang while she worked. Gospels. Maybe she had been trying, too, to have faith when everything around her said it wasn't possible.

Women used to die young, and didn't have much time to think about the nature of the world. Maybe that had been a good thing.

"You're pretty quiet today, Oida. You sure you didn't hurt yourself?"

"Just practicing not talking so much. You can't have it both ways."

"I'd plug that hole up," Janey said, carrying her plate to the sink. "I'd plug it up with rocks, too."

"No, you wouldn't. What if somebody did that to you?"

When they left, Oida cleaned the few dishes, and dried her hands. She took the pen hanging by the calendar, and thought about how she should write this down. She didn't want to put the word "hell" in her own handwriting. She could feel the heat of the sun streaming through the window onto her back. She wrote, "I know and he knows I do." Then she went outside. She could smell the honeysuckle that covered the storm cellar. Tiny green apples hung from a gnarled, stunted tree she had planted when her boy was fifteen and raging all the time. Purple hollyhocks lined the south side of her property. A dull brown redbird, a female, streaked a warning to whatever was nearby. "Good for you," Oida said. The air was so hot, so still and humid, like the moment was pendent in time, everything waiting on either side, before and after, and Oida knew right where she was.

# ⊰An Intimate Gesture⊱

The sun, sharpened by window glass, formed a rosy haze throughout the living room. It made both the occupants feel simultaneously languid and excited, though neither indicated so to the other. Above them, just below the ceiling, floated thin, wispy layers of cigarette smoke. Usually that annoyed him, and he suffered it as a price of her visits, but today he liked even the smoke. It reminded him of an old Bogart movie, of sharp wits and hungry minds and bodies. He was pleased that his apartment, in spite of his condition, could have this warm, romantic atmosphere. She, too, liked the room better today than ever before, and wondered that just a little sun could invert the world this way. She felt warm toward him, indulgent. Usually she was unpleasantly edgy when near him, because he was smarter than she and because he had no control over his disability. She was frightened by anything that could overtake a person.

"You know what I'd like?" he said, turning his wheelchair so his back was to the window, his face toward her. "I'd like you to wash my hair."

"Why?"

"Just because I'd like it."

"I don't think so," she said.

"Why not?"

"I don't want to."

"Thanks." He pushed a button on the arm of the wheelchair and zoomed toward the kitchen area. "I haven't had coffee yet. You have time for that, surely."

"I'll help."

"Nope."

She crushed the cigarette in the saucer he had given her for an ashtray, then followed him. She was a tiny woman, too thin, with long, unruly, reddish hair worn down and swinging. She wore jeans and a silk blouse, white tennis shoes. She knew she was pretty, and sometimes felt ashamed of knowing it or caring. She was particularly ashamed now, because of his twisted body. He would have been a good-looking man if something hadn't wracked him like that, something he had been born with. Muscular dystrophy? Multiple sclerosis? He wouldn't name it for her. He just said his father had it, and his sister, and now it had him and would see that he never died on his feet. If he were a healthy man, he would be tall, maybe even strong. He had big bones, and they all showed. The flesh was withering away, and one day a skeleton could sit in that chair and still be him. Maybe even still be alive.

He had difficulty filling the pan of water because he was angry now. He had only limited use of both arms—his right was the strongest—and if he tensed too much, he could do nothing but flop them around like damaged wings. He had the pan in his lap, had maneuvered the faucet extension hose from the sink to the pan, and needed to clamp the tube shut the moment there was enough water. "Don't watch me," he said.

"I wasn't."

"Yes, you were. Stop it." He shut the clamp, let the hose hang against the cabinet, and turned the chair slowly toward the stove, holding the pan on both knees. His left thumb was in the water. He couldn't help that.

"Maybe I should just go home," she said. "We're starting off wrong here. This isn't going to be a very good day."

"Don't go." He hated saying it, having said it. He both wanted her gone and wanted her here. "It's no big thing. I just felt insulted."

"I could feel insulted, you know. No one's ever asked me to do that kind of thing."

He laughed, a rough little chortle, and knew the pan was going to spill. He let it go rather than try to save it and end up with his pants drenched to the groin. The miniature wave swept black grounds across the yellow tile.

"I'll get it," she said, and he let her. When she knelt, he watched the round upside-down heart of her hips, the straight slender thighs. Many, many hands had traced those lines. If he could move, he'd cup those hips, and she'd laugh. She went to bed with people, she had said, as a gesture of friendship. "If they want to, and I want to, why not?"

"I didn't know touching me would be so repulsive to you," he said. "How can you be friends with me and feel that way?"

"I don't feel that way. You're making it up and pushing it on me. It's how you feel about you. Not me."

125

He liked that. "Is that true?" he said. "Really?"

"Yes." She threw soiled paper towels in the trash, took a fresh one to dry the floor. "It's a good thing you got rid of your dog," she said. "You had to clean up like this all the time, didn't you?"

"Yes, I did. It wasn't easy. But then, nothing is."

She put on more water and fixed the coffee while he returned to the living room. She heard music, his kind of music. Jazz. To her, it was frenetic and discordant. But then, he had to find life wherever he could, had to make it, like a little devil making his damnation just a bit more homey. She rolled her eyes again. "Jesus," she mouthed. She cleaned the top of the stove while she waited for the water to boil, carefully lifting the metal gratings so he wouldn't hear the barest whisper of her helping him this way. She pushed the trash down to the bottom to leave room for another day or two. She thought of trying to wash his hair, of holding that fragile skull, looking down into blue, sad eyes so close she'd never get away from them.

"And then we go to the park," she called. "Right? Coffee, then the park."

Silence. In the living room he wanted to say, "Go home, please. Get out of my house." He thought he should have enough pride to say that. He waited, though, to see if asking her to leave was really what he wanted. He might as well please himself. She was doing so. He didn't even want her to shampoo him, and he was sorry he had asked. He didn't see how just touching him could be so repulsive. She had slept with many men. They had talked about her lovers, matter-of-factly, as they had talked about his rigorous determination to care for himself as long as possible. "Each thing I give up," he had told her, "is forever gone, never retrievable. I can't go back."

"But that's true about anybody," she had said. "Any choice at all can take you down the garden path."

Now she carried cups into the living room, waited while he slid the desk-board up and over the arms of the chair. She put his cup down, then sat on the sofa again. She lighted a cigarette, and he looked away.

"I told you I won't smoke in here if it bothers you."

"Have your cigarette."

"I'm not going to stay here," she said, "if this continues. There's no reason for you to be mad at me because I won't wash your hair."

"It's a damned little thing to ask."

They drank without speaking for awhile, looking out the wide window. Jazz perked through the still-bright room. The sun was higher now, glazing crazy circles on the glass. He found them hypnotic, like being inside a burst of some kind. She momentarily closed her eyes against the glare, and yellow globes swam inside her lids. She knew when he lifted the cup and bent his head toward it. When she lighted a second cigarette from the first, he said, "Do you always do exactly what you want?"

"If I can," she said. "Why not?"

"To acquire discipline. To sharpen pleasure when it does come."

For a moment, they both thought she was leaving. She glanced at her purse, snubbed out the cigarette. She met his eyes. It was a trait she had always required of herself and one he admired.

"I am your friend," she said. "I just have faults like anyone does."

"I know."

"You wouldn't be so touchy if you'd get another dog. Get a big one, one that won't hop on you all the time."

"I can't pet them. Not really."

She studied her shoes. Her hair fell down, reddish amber.

Some men, he thought, could spread their fingers through it, comb it down, lift it.

"You have beautiful hair," he said.

She thought he had a nice voice. Looking down as she was, she'd never know he was twisted. She spoke toward the floor. "So. Where's the shampoo?"

"Just let it go."

"No. Where is it? Bathroom?"

He nodded.

"Do I shampoo you in there?"

"No. At the kitchen sink, if you're going to do it. We can manage me better."

She left the room. The music stopped. He rewound the tape, aware that she had returned and was waiting on him. "I've got some blues," he said, "if you want to look for the tapes."

"Not now. Not in the mood for blues."

"Not yet," he said, and forced a laugh. "But after this chore you might be."

"What are you doing?"

"Taking off my shirt. I don't want to get soaked." He tilted his head. "Want to help me?"

"You said you hate help."

He managed, in small jerks, to move his right hand near the top button. His pale, slender fingers fumbled, then caught the fabric.

128

She was by his chair immediately, quickly undoing each button. He leaned sideways, first one way, then the other, while she slipped the shirt free of his arms. Her long hair fell forward. He opened his mouth against it. She stepped back.

"Okay," she said. "To the sink."

"You roll me in there."

"You can do it yourself."

"You don't have to shampoo me at all, if you don't want to."

"I may not."

He pressed the power button, spun his chair around, and zoomed toward the kitchen.

He waited, facing the sink. His skin was smooth and unblemished, but his shoulder blades jutted like broken, mismatched wings, and his spine curved deeply inward at the waist.

"Your skin is pretty," she said.

"You thought I'd be white and pasty, right? Sluggish?"

"Cut it out."

He wheeled the chair around, reversed it till the tires were against the cabinet. "I have thin hair," he said. "Not even a thick mass to sink your fingers into."

"But it's a nice color, like pale wheat. And it's shiny. You have really healthy hair."

"Yes. I've been told that before."

He leaned back and closed his eyes.

"Tell me," she said, "if the water's too hot or cold."

"I will. Don't worry."

She massaged the suds into his scalp. It was a pink scalp, as fragile as she had feared, and the wet strands turned dark, thinner, like scraps of hair, rags of hair. She was sorry he couldn't even have thick hair, not even that.

Her blouse fell against his face. He could see the strip of lace topping each bra cup, the slight swell. Her breasts would be flattish and springy. He could feel the left one almost touching his mouth. Almost. He could smell the perfumy soapiness of her deodorant. He wished she were more intellectual. He wondered if she knew she wasn't. She was smart, but that wasn't the same thing. Her hands had a rhythm, like she had done this many times, maybe years of times. He could float forever on those hands. She stopped.

"I always shampoo at least twice," he said.

"How do you do it? Alone, I mean."

"It isn't easy."

"How?"

"I sit in the shower on a board across the tub, and I dab what soap I can on my head and let the water do the rest."

"I'm sorry."

"Don't be."

She sluiced the suds into the sink. Some dripped to the floor. She knelt with a paper towel to wipe it up. When she stood, she tested the water again.

"It's really nice outside," she said. "So bright and no wind."

She directed the water to his scalp, rinsed the thin hair.

"I wish you'd take your blouse off," he said. "Be sort of equal."

Outside a hollyhock bloomed deep red. A bumblebee flew heavily and lazily away.

"No," she said.

"I wish you would."

She pressed the water from his hair and dried his forehead. She stepped back. His head was braced against the rim of the sink, his hair like brown seaweed stranded on a pale stone. His mouth was lax. His eyes peered at her from lids almost closed.

"That was a sick dog you had," she said. "It wasn't a good choice for you. You need a dog that doesn't want to go out much, that likes lying around. I could help you house-train one, if you got a puppy. I'd even clean up the mess."

"Nope. If I can't care for it, I don't want it."

"You didn't give it enough treats. Did you know that? You have to give them more than they want, so they feel secure."

"Don't tell me how to do things, and I won't tell you. You don't have to go to bed with every man you know."

"If I want to, I do."

"Yes, I know. If you want to."

"Damn," she said. She could see his collarbones, his ribs, little steps up the frame of his body. All those spaces and gaps of what might have been. She stalked to the low shelves and read the tapes till she found one she recognized. She removed the jazz and clicked in blues. She crossed back, unbuttoning her blouse. She placed it next to her purse.

Now he was afraid to look directly at her. The room had changed, the air thick, smoky, the sunlight dusky.

She somehow seemed more clothed than ever. Her collarbones were very prominent, knotty at her shoulders. Her nipples were dark shadows beneath the sheer bra. He felt slightly shamed. "Actually," he said, "I wish you would shampoo me naked."

"Which of us? You?"

"Both."

"I don't think so."

She slipped her left hand beneath his head again, lifted the bottle of shampoo, poured a thin stream across his scalp, then lathered it slowly. The suds were light and airy. They made thick white swirls at her touch. A slow blues thrummed, and she moved her hands in time. "Do you ask every woman to shampoo you?"

"No."

"But others have, right?"

"Yes."

"And her? The one you slept with?"

"Not slept. We didn't sleep, so that's not quite accurate."

"She washed your hair?"

"No. If she had, we might have stayed together."

"She wasn't worth staying with."

"No. You're right." He wished he had never told her about the one woman, his one truly sexual encounter. He had traded it as conversation in kind, when they first became friends. How was he to know her experiences would continue to unfold while his had been offered, used up, gone, withered and limited as himself?

He felt like a victim twice over, victim of the woman who had lain in his bed as if his limbs could move, as if he could volunteer pleasure for her, and victim of this one who had taken his encounter as an anecdotal exchange instead of as a turning point in a down-sloping life. "I would never have asked her," he said. "She wasn't like you."

"How not like me? Not as loose?"

"Not as warm. You're a warm woman."

"No, I'm not. I said no."

"You said it to my face. You didn't go away and never call again."

"You called her."

"Yes, and she was always busy. She should have simply stated that she didn't want to come here anymore."

"You could have asked."

"No, I couldn't. You know that. I'm the one who can't function. That's as blatant as I should have to get. If I have to bring it up as well, I'm doubly naked. With her, everything was reduced to sex. A shampoo is more intimate than sex."

Her fingers spread over his scalp, pressing the water back. She rested his head against the sink. "Now the rinse," she said. She dried her hands, hesitated. Then she removed her bra. She slipped her shoes off and unbuttoned her belt. She slid the jeans down and off, folded them on the arm of the sofa. She removed her underpants, laid them on the jeans.

He didn't want to have to ask. She knew that.

He tried to shift his weight to help her. She had to get on her knees to pull his slacks and undershorts from beneath his buttocks.

"The backs of my thighs have eruptions," he said.

"I didn't notice."

"From the constant sitting."

133

"Anyone could have them."

She folded his clothing next to hers.

"You are," he said, "very beautiful."

"So are you."

"Do you mean that?"

"Yes." She removed the cap from the rinse bottle. "I think I do. You're whole-person beautiful."

"You mean who I am, not just my body."

"Yes." She cupped his head again. "There's a lovely hollyhock outside this window," she said.

"I know. It's right by the walk. There's a peach tree farther down. We should sit out there later. Have coffee. While my hair dries."

"You do want it, you know. Sex. And you pretend you don't."

"No. I don't want it. My body doesn't feel that kind of desire."

"Yes, it does. It has to. It's a human body."

"Maybe I killed the desire, from knowing that it was never possible."

"You didn't kill it. You hid it. Women don't like secret things, motives. That's why she never came here again."

"I have no secrets from you, especially motives."

"Maybe they're secret from you, too."

The rinse was sleek, unnaturally smooth. Her touch was too brief. Her breasts pressed his face fleetingly. Once his lips brushed a dark circle, and she held still a moment. He tasted her. Then she pulled away, dried his hair, stood free.

"So," she said, meeting his eyes only briefly. "Done."

"No."

The sun warmed the room again, grew brighter as if a filmy cloud had passed on.

"No?"

"Not yet. Don't be done yet."

She shrugged. "What more?"

"I don't know."

His hands lay useless at his groin. She looked away, toward the living room window, then the kitchen. He believed she did so to allow him to study her, and he was right. She didn't know what she should do now. She wanted to go home, to be home, never to have been here at all. She thought she was a cold woman. She wished she didn't have to know this about herself.

He thought she was perhaps too fair. Her veins lay close to the surface. "You're absolutely beautiful," he said. "You are the most beautiful thing I have ever seen in my whole life."

"Don't say that."

"It's true. You're more lovely than any idea I've ever had."

"Oh God," she said. "Okay. Okay." She grabbed the shampoo bottle.

"Don't make me feel bad," he said. "I'd rather you didn't do anything if you don't want to."

She dampened her hands, poured the liquid into her right palm. She began at his neck. She moved both hands over him, smoothing the soap like a lotion. He closed his eyes. She dampened her hands again, poured more shampoo. She sudsed only the front of him, but entirely. She touched his genitals as she did his arms and chest. Her hands were quick and firm. Then she moistened the towel and rinsed him twice.

"There," she said. "Done again. Do you want the same clothes on?"

"Don't stop. It's wonderful."

"It's over."

"It's the most wonderful . . ."

She grabbed her clothing, dressed in jerky movements.

He wheeled to the sofa, managed to grasp his shorts.

"I'll help," she said. "Just wait a minute."

"I can do it."

"I said just wait a minute."

He did so. She bent to lift his feet one at a time and slide the shorts up. He pressed his shoulders against the back of the chair to raise his body slightly. She did the same with his slacks. She seemed surer now how to maneuver the clothes and him.

"I don't want this to have harmed our friendship," he said, and he meant it exactly as deeply, as roughly and hoarsely, as he had said it.

"I wouldn't have done it if I hadn't wanted to. "

"No. You wouldn't have. I know that about you."

She put one of his arms into the shirt sleeve, eased the shirt behind him and then onto the other arm. She buttoned it.

"You're very good at this," he said.

"I'll hang the towels in the shower."

She left the room. He whirled his chair to the large window. The sun glowed a clear summer day with only the morning gone. "I should get some new clothes," he called.

She reentered the room, took a cigarette from her purse.

"Don't," he said, "be upset about this."

She didn't answer.

"You are, aren't you? Upset?"

"I think so."

"I am, too. I wish I hadn't asked. But I couldn't let it go once you said no. You made it important. You made it the most important thing in the world."

"You should never have brought that dog home from the pound."

"Why do you keep talking about the damned dog? It wasn't my fault. I wanted to keep it. I tried to keep it. It didn't want me. If it could have taken me back to the pound, it would have. Get it straight."

"I got it straight. I don't like any of this."

"You don't like me. That's what it boils down to."

"Well, you don't like me, either."

"And that's right. True as rain. True as past come home again."

They looked at one another. She lifted one hand as if saying, So much for that. He found it touching. He thought perhaps she felt like crying. She looked as if she did.

"I'm sorry," he said. "I've got a mean mouth."

"Your whole family has this, don't they?"

He nodded. "Father and sister. Mother's free."

She picked up her purse.

He wheeled toward the door. "Why did you ask?"

"I don't know."

"Yes, you do."

"No. And I don't want to."

"You ask questions for the hell of it?"

"Why not? You do." She opened the front door. She

felt relief the moment she did so. The air seemed to rush in, envelop her, draw her outside, immediately, now.

He wanted to follow, in exactly those steps, in exactly her mood, whatever it was. "Put yourself in my place," he said. "Just think about it for awhile before you decide anything, before you act."

"Okay."

"You don't mean that. But please do. Maybe I haven't behaved well, but I've had good intentions. I wanted something more between us. Nothing ugly, just more. It's natural."

"I know that. I know it's natural. I'm not behaving very well, either."

She went back in, and he waited at the end of the ramp.

"I washed the saucer," she said. She raised a white bag. "And got the trash. Save you a trip."

"I can take it out, you know."

"I know."

"The shampoo was perfect. A real exchange, an intimate gesture."

"You need a tree of some kind in front. The light glares in there."

"A little. It's not bad. Don't be angry."

"Anyone would be willing to do that for you."

"Would they? Anyone?"

"If you asked them. If it were gradual."

"I hate to ask."

"You asked me."

"We're friends. We've been friends a long time."

"Yes."

They were both afraid. Both felt delicate, as if a word

or a gesture would throw them into the rest of their lives before they were ready.

"Let me have that trash bag," he said. "I can take it. I do it all the time."

"I've got it." She crossed to the bin, came back. Her hair seemed wild to him.

"We could do the park later this afternoon," he said. "After you finish your work."

"I don't know." She thought his voice was reedy. It faded away in the open air.

He wondered why she always mumbled, just coasted along.

He whirred beside her, down the walk, across the gravel. His chair lurched. He stopped. "You're the only one who has washed my hair. The only one." He was tilting his head toward her. He tried to hold it steady, but couldn't. He was ashamed of himself for caring what she did or what she thought.

"Is that true?" she asked.

"Yes. Does that matter?"

"Maybe." She got in the car. "No," she said. "It doesn't matter."

"You're not coming back, are you?"

"Sure, I am." She started the motor.

"No, you're not. I can tell."

She put the car in gear. "I guess you know better than I do."

"Why would you say that?"

"I don't know. I'm sorry." She pursed her lips as if to blow a kiss toward him, but didn't. "You didn't feel a thing, did you? Not really."

He started to say yes he had, but he knew they weren't speaking of the same feeling. "No," he said. "I didn't."

"That's what I thought."

"It was still wonderful."

"See you later," she said.

"Later."

He watched her drive away. Then he turned to his yard, the chair motor humming. He hurried to the hollyhock, to the peach, then to the front again. He looked at the empty driveway, then quickly went up the ramp into his living room. He parked his chair before the wide window. He thought perhaps she might come back, might drive up and come striding across his yard, up to his door. He felt sleepy and oddly agitated. He hunched his shoulders and concentrated to fling his hands, to spread his arms as wide as he could. Then he closed his eyes. He felt the heat soothing his face, torso, his limbs. She stopped at the first light, and someone honked for her to get out of the way. She drove around the block, down the alley, and by his apartment. She couldn't bring herself to look toward his window. She was afraid he'd be there, looking desperate and unhappy or desperate and happy. She thought the intensity might blind her. She drove away, toward the afternoon. He fell asleep and dreamed disturbing, opulent dreams.

# ⊰ Friday Fishermen ⊱

The old men of Buxton who still fished liked to sit on the east side of the river, just at sunset. The heat and glare made them slightly uncomfortable, but fishing wasn't *meant* to be comfortable: with sweat and a bit of labor, they coaxed fish to their hooks and lures. Directly across the river, a steep bank covered with trees and bared roots would have afforded them shade, but then the descent would be risky, and the ascent really taxing. Only a few people fished the west side. They did, though, catch some big ones.

This Friday—because the old men liked Fridays best, just a few hours before the Willard Bros. station fish fry—they were astonished to see a heavy woman making her way down the west slope. She was at least two hundred pounds, and since she was also fairly tall, as far as their perspective allowed them to determine size, she might have been even three hundred. In one hand she held a tackle box, in the other a rod. She used the rod like a staff to help her purchase steps down the hill. She was a long time reaching the bottom, and the men's enjoyment was mixed with dread that they might have to assist. A lone woman falling down a steep bank meant hard rescue. And they weren't young, no more than she was light.

But she didn't fall. Reaching level ground, she brought forth a folding stool which they assumed had been fastened somehow to her back, placed it a few feet from the water's edge, lowered her massive self down till the stool disappeared, and leaned precariously to one side to open her tackle box. She proceeded to bait the hook.

No one recognized her, though each conjectured.

"That's Elvira Hayes from Cottondale."

"No, it's not. She's got too much hair."

"Jimmy Hargrove's mother. She's the one with dropsy, likes to fish. I heard about her."

"Hargrove's mother was in the hospital last week. I doubt she'd be fishing this week."

The catfishers set their lines. One lit a cigarette, and the smoke rose lazily and heavily, finally just leveled out in the humidity. Across the water, the woman sat in shadow, though the sun still hovered at the crest of her hill. Her line was in shadow, too, as if the hook lowered into deeper and perhaps more richly stocked water.

"Bet she's after bass."

"That's a good spot."

"She's using a hook. I don't see her reeling anything in."

"She is huge, isn't she?"

"God, her line snapped! See that? Damn! She's got something big!"

The other men watched, too, glancing away just for quick looks at their own lines, which surely would tauten up any second, any second, because that's how it happened.

She leaned back, pulled, reeled, leaned back, pulled, reeled, and finally up it came, an arching silver-gray whopping little thing.

"Bass!"

"Good one."

Was she looking at them? Did she care that they approved of her?

"Mighty fine fishing!" one of them whooped toward the woman. "That's a doozy!"

Maybe she heard? Did she smile?

One of the men, who favored overalls only on Fridays, and who today also had on a favorite blue flannel shirt, though it was meant for cooler weather, said, "I'm gonna put out another line, with some liver."

"If they're not biting one thing, they're not likely to another."

A line went flat, and the overalled man dropped the new pole, ran for the one now in the water, jerked it up. A yellow flat fish slapped the sky a hundred times.

"Perch."

"Can't get away from 'em."

"Wish they'd go to the other side of the river."

They liked the woman right then. She was fine. Sort of sturdy, a good old country woman. She had probably lived in this area all her life, a farmer's wife, maybe widowed now. She was no pretentious thing, certainly. That was a cotton dress; her shoes were flat, practical, meant to keep her on her feet and nothing else. And she liked fishing. She was darn good at it, too.

The sun went lower. They got, among them, three

catfish, and six perch. The latter they threw back in. One, though, was so tiny that the catfish hook made both eyes bulge. They certainly couldn't remove the hook, and leaving it in to dissolve—which the new hooks would do—was still a death sentence, because the creature couldn't eat.

"They don't feel pain, though," one man said. He was a burly fellow, almost seventy-five, with skin so red he looked like he might spontaneously burn up, as some of the area legends indicated could actually occur. He said the redness came from a medication, but the other men didn't really believe that, since the man's father had also been a red color. And the sister, who lived near the Bluff and who had had nine children, was a bluish color. The family had something odd in their history.

The woman caught another bass. This time, because of the lower sun and the almost night on her side of the lake, the men couldn't be sure of the size or the color, but the fact that it had taken so long to reel it in, and that the rod had been almost straight out for awhile, meant she had a monster on the line.

"I'd like to know what she's using."

"Go ask her."

"Oh yeah. I'm going to hike over there and down the hill to ask."

"Yell it out. I'll do it."

"Don't you do it." The first fellow glared as if he would, if near enough, clamp a restraining hand on the other's shoulder. "If I want something, I can ask for it myself."

"She's probably using bread balls. My granny could

catch anything with one of them, catfish, bass, crappie, gar."

"Nobody wants a gar."

"There's use for them."

"What use? Even chickens don't want 'em."

"Medicine of sorts."

"For what?"

"I don't know. I told you it was my grandmother caught gar. She had a purpose."

"Your grandma, I take it, was a witch."

"Don't go kidding around like that. She was a good Christian woman."

"This is Friday."

"What's that got to do with anything?"

"Well, maybe that woman over there needs to eat fish because it's Friday."

"Then she's not from around these parts."

"Oh, come off it. There's a Catholic church over at the Bluff, another at the Cape."

"The Whore of Babylon."

"Let's put church off till Sunday, what say?"

They agreed without saying anymore about it. The sun, from behind the hill, was casting a red glow, and it flamed up like maybe something was burning inside the hill, on the outside of which sat the woman, placidly, still fishing.

"You say you know her?"

"No. I just think she's from around here."

"There's the state institution not too far. How do you know she's not from there?"

"Why would she be here? If she ran away, she'd be

gone. And she wouldn't have a rod with her. People don't escape with rods."

"They do if they're pistols. Ha!" That was from a skinny man, good farmer, who wore jeans and nice starched shirts, and cowboy boots because he was short. He was known for being able to call square dances and to use a bullwhip. He could also serve as an auctioneer, though he didn't believe he was any good at it.

"Did you hear something?" he said. "Something real high and keening?"

"Nope."

"I did a minute ago. Like a dog baying."

"Sharper."

"High bay, real long and mournful."

They all fell silent. A slight evening breeze had picked up, and it waved over the water, made the surface seem as if it were running toward the other bank, then scurrying back.

"Now I hear it."

"What in the hell is that?"

"It's her."

"Her?"

"Yeah. Listen."

They fell silent again, two of them with heads down as if they couldn't see and hear at the same time.

"Is she singing?"

"That's no normal tune. Nothing like I've heard."

"Maybe we should call it quits."

"I don't want to go to the fish fry with no more than we got."

"We don't have to go."

"We could toss away what we have, just show up."

"My catfish are decent, and I'm not throwing 'em back."

"It doesn't matter. There's always enough fish."

"This might be a night when nobody caught any."

"Except maybe her."

"That's what I meant."

They packed up, a little belligerently. The shadow of the hill now covered them, and the breeze was cool. One line had snagged, and the man cut it loose. The free, silky line waved up like it would fly away, then fell down the guideholes and dragged in the grass behind him. Another man wrapped foil around the hook and the rod, pressed it to keep the two together.

They had come in two vehicles, trucks, two men in each front seat and the others in the back. They resumed their positions, and the smoker again lighted up. He coughed twice, and his companions looked superior for a moment. Then one rapped on the cab window.

"Let's drive over to the top of the hill. She's moving up."

That she was. She's wasn't totally visible, but the whiteness of her thick thighs could be seen below the dark dress, and her fleshy arms marked her width.

"Think she can make it up that hill?"

"If she can't, she'll have to spend the night, because I couldn't move her."

"She wouldn't fish down there if she couldn't get back up."

"Sure she would. They haven't got any sense."

"I'd rather you didn't talk about her right now."

"Afraid she'll hear us?"

In the other truck, talk was in a similar vein, eyes on

the target going up the slope, until down-hanging branches hid her from their view. The men drove their trucks at a decent slow pace, not enough to raise much dust, up the dirt road, and turned onto the top of the hill. They switched off the motors.

When she didn't appear right away, a younger man said, "She's not going to show herself with a bunch of guys waiting for her."

The men agreed, without much talk. After all, violence happened to women all the time, maybe not to women who looked like her, but women were afraid of the possibility. That was part of woman nature. A good part. That woman knew her position, and they were her caretakers. They didn't discuss this. They looked at the various leaves, identifying some, remembered times they'd been here before, thought of a pain they'd had recently, or an unpaid bill, but their thoughts came back to the path's end, right before them, and the woman who wouldn't appear.

"She'll go around the long way."

"Should we go see?"

"No. Why? That'd scare her, too."

"It would scare me. I think we should head back, go on to the fish fry."

"That's 'cause you have fish. Let's wait a minute more."

The sun now had lowered even on this side of the hill, just a rounded tip visible through thousands of trees, and it was sinking. It made one of the men remember a hymn, and he hummed and sang one line: "My earthly sun is sinking fast, my day is almost done."

"That's supposed to be 'My race is almost run.'"

Just then the woman appeared. She was truly huge, as tall as the tallest of them, and very broad. Her breasts were huge, too, and sloped down to her waist. Beneath the hem of her dress, her legs were stark white and her feet large and muddy, the black shoes coated in a brown that wasn't like earth but like something a little cruder.

"Thought you might need help," the skinny man in jeans and a starched shirt and cowboy boots said, and she didn't respond in words or movement. She just stayed by the line of rocks that marked off the drive-in area. Her right hand held the handle of the tackle box. Her left hand held her rod midway and held also a line with five fish still alive and wet.

"That's a good haul," the red man said.

"They weren't biting on our side," another man said.

Something coughed. From somewhere came a hooting sound, but not really like an owl. The woman didn't move.

The air was charged, like the sun had taken itself and heat and color but left something very high and dancing right there in the air. It was in their heads, and their lungs, and on their skin, and they might have been able to shape it into something real.

But the woman, with no sign that she was going to act at all, opened her mouth and let out a high, strong, mournful, wonderful note that she sustained, and sustained, and sustained. It didn't echo. It didn't fade. It just was. She was so huge, old or getting there, dressed godawful, feet like she was turning into clay or something worse, but she just held onto that note. When it ended, real suddenly, still at full force, she just looked at them somberly, as if she were in the split second before the sound. And they were there, too. The drivers started their trucks at the same time. One backed out in the other's wake. One man put his cap on and then reseated it, which might have been a disguised acknowledgment of the woman left on the hill.

They zoomed down the dirt road, dust rising to filter the night behind them, past their own fishing site, and up toward town.

"She had a remarkable voice. I mean, it was crazy what she did, but that was a nice voice."

"Strong one, for sure."

"Why you think she did that?"

"Who knows? It worked."

"Worked for what?"

"I don't know. She did it, we left."

"We were leaving anyhow."

"I know. Something acts crazy, it scares normal people away."

"So she's from that institution, you think?"

"Hey! Did you guys see a car up there?"

No one had. No vehicle.

"There's no houses in that area. Where'd she come from?"

"Maybe somebody let her out. Maybe they're coming back for her."

They conjectured, each to himself, while they talked about Willard's fish fry, about cornbread, about beer or coffee. Town was only a few minutes away, but they noticed that the moon had become quickly visible and it was a thick moon, very white, sluggish, sitting right on top of Buxton itself. Later, as they ate and drank together, in the weekly communion of the men of Buxton, they talked about how dead the river had been, nothing biting, the wind getting cool so quickly. They were each married, and they were each glad the wives never attended the Friday-night event. They liked thinking about going home later, maybe, later, after another beer or so, after a little more comfort with the fellows, and then, then, they'd hit the long, dark road home.

# ⊰ Late Fall ⊱

My name is **Esther Wheeler**. I live in the first-floor rooms of a house that was built in the 1880s and in which my family lived and died. I'm the last generation, Esther Wheeler who never married, never left home, whose house gathers slender children to the yard where they guess at monsters and ghosts, make tales to liven their lives in this town. Sometimes I stand in my doorway with the screen between me and them, and the children gasp and run. I am wraithlike. The frailty of the woman in my mirror astonishes me. I know her bones are brittle, the loose, draping skin a delicate sheath between life and death. A skeleton lies under there, a somewhat painful one.

My house sits at the junction of a gravel side street. That road dips down, up, snakes to houses newer than mine, ends at an old church worn grayer than I. My neighbor, Oida, whose house is on the corner across from mine, a higher corner, used to attend that church. One summer she crossed the road a few times to urge me to attend with her. She offered to drive me there and back. She had only learned to drive that year, had been given a black car with a curved top and fenders, only two doors. That car scared her, I know. She drove it in inches, not miles. Her children were gone then, and the car a sign of their caretaking. They were fond of her, but she had raised them not to need anything, and they were a little blind to others' needs. When they were small, she sent them here on holidays, delivering a paper plate with slices of roast or pieces of chicken, and always a sweet. I could imagine her kitchen each night, warmth steaming the windows. She worked at the factory then, with a husband more gone than home. He left one year for good.

Oida kept getting on her roof this fall. The first day I saw her up there, a month ago, she wore dark slacks, heavy shoes, and a man's black coat, wool probably, left over from the husband or her one son. Her hair is curly, and it bobbed wild in the late fall wind. She was a pretty woman when young, and still is to some eyes, my eyes. We older women see beauty even in the deepness of lines, the shape of them, that they fanned into smiles, see beauty even in the fold of skin from a fine jaw, a strong face. We see, perhaps, what we must see.

One fall Oida bought all the books that had been stored in my attic, decades of books from great-aunts who were teachers. I had read most of them, in my kind of twilight youth, more past than growing. My mother was dying most of my childhood. Oida thought her children might read their way to gentility and goodness. She didn't say that. She rambled, as was her way, about their lives being so limited, so dreary, with their father having the nature he did. He had a traveling, drinking, bellicose nature. Oida didn't say that. I did, and she shrugged and lifted one more box of books. Dust puffed out, and sunlight caught the fragile clouds. Everything seemed lighter when Oida was around.

The second morning she wore a stocking cap, and she could have been Quasimodo faltering across the roof. Her back is humped from bending over the factory machines so many years. She climbed from the high pitch to the roof on the room they added for her son. She removed the screening on the attic vent and peered inside. That's when I knew she was looking not for a leak, but for a creature. Something was caught in the top of her house. She did things like that, maintenance work, though her son lived just minutes away. In the summer, she would mow, put out a garden, spray pesticide. Once she went down to the drainage ditch at the end of her lot and cut away the growth.

I can't move like that. I'm eighty to her sixty, and I'm brittle.

Two of her children came that first weekend. Her son, named James, got on the roof. The daughter stood next to Oida in the yard. Both of them had their arms folded beneath their breasts, looking up. Their voices carried to my kitchen window. Oida didn't believe it was a squirrel. No. She shook her head at that. The son said he could put out a trap. But he didn't, not then. He didn't do much at all, just squat down, listening to Oida, and smiling. He has a nice smile; all her children do. He has a mellow, booming voice, strong as a man's should be, like he knows what he's saying and that alone should provide for Oida.

He did put a trap up there, the next weekend. Oida watched him, silently, shaking her head. That gesture must always have served as her greatest resistance. She made no other that I know of, though windows aren't enough to know a life, anymore than are visiting children, mute, moving from their mother's will and not their own. Her James laughed as he crossed toward the ladder, pointed at the pecan tree. When her children left, Oida came outside two or three times, staring up at the roof, then at the pecan tree that always drew squirrels, as if deciding whether or not to leave the trap. Her backyard has more trees than the rest of the yards on this street put together. She moved the little ones from time to time, and they never died.

A few days ago I banged my hand on a skillet handle, and two fingers on my left hand are broken. I know what this is. It runs in my mother's family. I have lived this long because I have not pressed myself beyond my strength or my endurance.

The town children who run from my house sometimes stopped at Oida's. She would guide them to the back where they would stand at the edge of the drainage ditch, or, in summer, walk the circumference of her garden. Sometimes she hosed off tomatoes or strawberries, and they ate together. She had apples, too, in fall.

When she took the trap down, it was empty. The day was ending, early, as it does when winter comes on. She tossed the trap to the ground below and edged to the yard-side roof. She disappeared, into the attic, I suppose. When she appeared again, she had a flashlight in her hand and tucked it into her coat pocket. Oida was no fool. She wouldn't have stumbled around inside a dark attic. She went back up there a little later. She spread seeds under each vent. She had a bird caught somewhere in her house. That's a bad sign, which Oida would know.

It means death, not just for the bird, but for someone near and dear.

Living alone and growing old isn't easy. One has to learn how to do it. Old houses don't heat well, and rooms are cold around the edges. Winds seep around windowsills, send drafts where none should be. Lights in every room give an illusion of warmth, of daylight, of an inside spring, I guess. Sometimes, when I'm pain free, and I doze into half-sleep, I forget my age, am startled at the sight of the veined hands on my lap. I think I was lovely once, too. Maybe I could have married, could have risked that welcome into my life. But no one came. Of course, no one ever left me, either. Oida wasted down to nothing the year he left her for good. That was in March. Her dresses hung on her frame like wilting petals. She sent the children here with a May basket, cookies and candies. The boy said it was a stupid girl thing. He was a pretty little boy. All her children were pretty. He stayed yards away, all dark angles like his father, twisting against being there. He didn't know what a blessing he had in his house.

My mother took ten years to die because people helped her stay alive. While her bones were being lightened, riddled, her eyes turned blacker and blacker. She was very young. But she raised me, she used to say. She saw me a woman first. One day I'll slip and lie there and ease away, unless someone like Oida notices the lights don't change, groceries aren't delivered. Oida has sharp eyes.

No one can sleep with a bird caught in the walls. The wings flutter like heartbeats, here, there, so frantic and fragile, so maddening that one would rip a wall apart to stop that sound. Perhaps Oida did. Inside that house, smaller than my own, maybe warmer, brighter, perhaps she peeled away wallpaper, used crowbar and hammer to pull back boards. Perhaps she gutted that house, each room, worked day and night. She would do that, to save a life.

Oida fell yesterday. She went up the ladder carefully, wearily, around to the attic entrance. When she returned she stood, head bowed, as if wondering what to do next, where to turn. Her hair was free, curly white. Long years ago, yesterday, it was red. She stepped toward the roof's edge, bent to grip the ladder post, and fell then, a smooth motion, continuous, though it couldn't have been, and wasn't, since her arms flailed and a sharp cry must have sped toward my window. I tried to run, I did run, from my kitchen, to the back door, down the steps, that pathetic scurry-run of old bones too late. I would have sped across the yard, would have leapt to catch her, save her, poor thing, Oida, poor small abused woman. But I stumbled at the first step down, and only my firm grip kept me from being prostrate and broken. I could see her crumpled, and I didn't want to see that fair face close up, be unable to raise her weight, carry her inside and sooth her brow. I went inside, up the narrow cool hall, and called the operator. Then I watched until the ambulance arrived.

I watched, too, when her children came. The daughter knocked on my door, but I didn't answer. I have no need to know more than I can bear. They left with suitcases, so I know Oida lies alive somewhere, around someone, will flutter hope and smiles some time longer. I watch for James, for the day he comes to close the house. If grief must come to someone, let it rustle the dark, calm carriage of her son.

Oida may not return, of course. That house may lie barren, still, forever empty yards from me. I'd like to think that in the spring, when children whisper on my walk, try to gaze inside the house, inside of me, that I will emerge on my porch, speak kind words, meander down a flowering walk and gather them in. But I won't. I've never been blind, not to Oida's needs or my own. When the days grow long again, and windows warm, and children come, I'll stand behind the screen, let them see me, let them quail and run, let them tell their stories, make their lives. I know Oida could have left that bird alone. Eventually the haunting sound would have ceased.

# ⊰With a Change of Seasons⊱

Frank Cauley loved to fish. Even before he retired at age sixty-three, he had tried to fish at least five days a week in the summer months. The Castor River was only a mile or so from the outskirts of Buxton, and Frank would rise early, putting in a couple of hours on the bank before driving back to change quickly and make it to the courthouse where he worked. Frank was the county treasurer, or had been the treasurer for ten years before the cancer. But fishing was still what he thought of first when he woke, not the other. That would come later, when Wilma walked around the kitchen with a long face, or when the pain burned and tore upward from his rectum deep into his body.

Frank pushed back the covers and sat on the edge of the bed. He could smell the heat from the living room furnace. Only September, but the days were already cool. In a few weeks Wilma would turn the heat up high the first thing in the morning and leave it that way, scooting around in her slippers with a sweater clutched to her chest. Summer was over. Across from him the edges of the window around the drapes were dark. It would be cloudy outside then, going to rain probably, and Wilma wouldn't go with him out to the river. She hadn't let him go alone ever since Dr. Massey had said cancer, as if it could suddenly take one big bite out of him and he'd drop into the river. What he could do, now, was tell Wilma he was going over to Dave's, do a little work on those cupboards they were putting in the kitchen. He could take his son's rod and spend the day on the banks. Frank stood and shed his pajamas slowly, drawing on the jeans and shirt he had folded on the chair the night before. He hadn't lost too much weight. He wondered how little he'd get.

"Morning," he said as he rounded from the hall toward the step-down bathroom in the storeroom, the only place they could fit it in when they had added the plumbing years ago. Wilma's eyes scanned him with her new expression before she smiled.

"You feel like eating?" she asked.

"Sure." He was going to eat every morning, want it or not. It made Wilma's face relax a little when he ate. In the bathroom he shaved his dark stubble and brushed his hair with the brush his grandson had given him for Christmas. His name was on the back in gold letters. Frank. There wasn't much hair to brush, but the bristles were soft and felt good against his scalp anyway. His skin seemed to have turned gray in the past few months, and he recognized the color. It wasn't the cancer. Just what happened to a fair-skinned person who hadn't been moving around enough to keep the blood going under his skin. He rubbed his face, even his forehead, before he went in the kitchen.

Wilma set the plate in front of him. The napkin was

there, the juice. Wilma had always done things right.
The window to his left showed the clouds dark and moving. Damn.

"How you feeling this morning?"

"Fine. I'm going over to Dave's. Feel like doing a little woodwork."

"You know you shouldn't be doing stuff like that. It
wears you out so."

"Does not."

Her sweater was dark blue, the cuffs stretched and
gaping around her wrists. Wilma didn't eat anything in
the mornings, and little the rest of the day. She still
watched her weight as she always had and was still a fine-
looking woman. There were creases in her skin, but not
bad ones. They had deepened lately. He wished she
wouldn't change, even if he had to.

"I wish you wouldn't go, Frank. Just stay around the
house. Rest up. Dr. Massey said . . ."

"I'm not taking any more of them anyhow."

Wilma turned the cup in its saucer. There was a part
down the middle of her hair, and the scalp was white, the
hair coiled smoothly as it had always been. "You're supposed to take the whole series," she said. "It won't do no
good if you don't take them all."

"Think Dave'd care if I did a little work on my own?"

"No," she said finally. Her eyes were black, small. She
loved him a lot, always had. He knew that.

"You coming home for lunch?" she asked.

"I'll get something out of their icebox."

He had a key to his son's house. He had helped build
that house, taking as much care with it as he had in raising his son. He liked his daughter-in-law, too. She was

161

a lot like Wilma. Quiet, soft-spoken, kept that house shining. Never said one word when he and Dave took off weekends fishing.

The problem was, Frank thought, as he took the dirt road leading back to the Castor, what if he caught something? He couldn't throw it away. A man couldn't do that, catch something just to catch it. That was whiling away time. Wasting things. He didn't do that, even if Wilma didn't like fish. She didn't like him scaling them in her backyard, either, but even Wilma admitted it was better than wasting them. Of course, the cat got a lot. The old black Tom, battered and mad all the time. It was fall now, and by rights the cat was Glenneth's, but Glenneth wouldn't mind a couple more weeks. It wouldn't be long before she had that cat forever anyway.

Poor Frank, Glenneth thought, as she saw the car leave the driveway. She knew about the cancer. Not from Frank, of course. In all the years they had lived side by side, he had been a good neighbor, never nosy, never complaining. He always just talked about the tomatoes in her garden being bigger than his, what kind of flower was that she was planting, things like that. Wilma had told her, sitting in the cluttered living room of Glenneth's house, weeping silently the day after the doctors had told her they couldn't see any reason to even open him up. "He says he won't take the treatments. Says they just drag it out, make you sicker. He's got to take those treatments, Glenneth, he's just got to." And he had, at first. Glenneth knew that from Wilma and from the fact she hadn't seen Frank taking off with his rod for a long time. Hadn't seen him puttering around his backyard, straightening the low fence Glenneth had built. Their lots stretched back to a drainage ditch and a barren hill beyond. Frank had said they didn't need a fence, but Glenneth had carefully planted her flower beds on her own side of the property line, bearing in mind Wilma's love of neatness, and had hammered little slats into the soil one day, just to make sure she kept it all straight.

Glenneth opened all the drapes in her house and regretted it wasn't sunnier. It was always nicer to start the day off with a little sunshine. She had five more minutes to get the kitchen in order, then she'd have to be off if she wanted to punch in on time. Glenneth had worked thirty-one years in the factory; four more and she could retire. She was round and rosy, loved large prints and wore them. Her house was filled with knickknacks, everything anyone had ever given her: from Christmases at the factory when they drew names and gave small gifts; from her sister, her nieces; even the things her own parents had saved. Glenneth had never married, never loved, unless she counted the boy back in high school. She had believed she would love somebody someday, and marry, but it hadn't happened. Time had kept going, and here she was fifty-nine, living in the same house she'd been raised in, with no one she really mattered to. But she was happy enough, she thought. She had her house and her garden and her job.

Glenneth set out the soup she would have when she came home for lunch, and stepped outside. "Tom?" she called. "Tom?" She could see him in Frank Cauley's backyard, curled up by the chopping block. "Tom, it's September, you old thing." He ignored her, face toward the block. "Suit yourself," she said, and entered the house again. Glenneth had never petted the cat. It owned the two lots, hers and Frank's. It disappeared at times, but it always returned, either at her door or Frank's, depending on the season.

"You seen old Tom?" Frank would call to her from his backyard. "Fed him this morning," she'd answer, and Frank would nod. Off and on through the winter months, the same question and answer. Then in summer, when Frank fished, the reverse. Her calling to him and his reassurance that the cat was okay.

Frank took the cushion from the trunk and put it in his favorite spot on the bank. He wished he had his peacoat. Wilma would have known right away, though, and would have been miserable all day. Now she wouldn't know till he got home, if he caught anything, that is. The day was changing, clouds still blowing fast, wind picking up. He dropped the line in the dark water. No more of the treatments. Driving down there, or rather, letting Wilma drive him. Fifty miles each way. Walking in for the first few days, then leaning on Wilma the others. Vomiting till he wished he'd die right then, right that minute. Pills for the nausea, pills to counteract the reaction that broke him out in red welts. Pills and pills and vomiting. No more. His grandson didn't like to fish, but that was okay. There was enough insurance for Wilma. If that lizard had come out for sunning, he was going to have a long wait. People would miss him. Dave. Wilma. He hadn't done anything good for anyone, maybe, but he hadn't hurt anyone, either. He'd been a good husband and father. Worked at the cleaners till he got the treasurer's job at the courthouse. Had his own teeth; he wouldn't look too bad, maybe, at the funeral. The lizard moved sluggishly away. Frank held the rod with one hand already bluish from the chill. He just watched the water, the dirt, the trees, wondered where the lizard had gone.

"Glenneth, could you stop by the office on break?" Mr. Phillips, the manager, was an old friend. Glenneth had known him all the years she worked in the factory. They'd had it out over a few things—piece-price goods, bad machines, bad lighting. That sort of thing. She was one of his best workers. She smiled at him now and nodded. He was a good man, a decent boss. Only once had he pulled in and balked, and that was over the fan. The factory was in a long, low building, non-union for years, and more capable of closing up completely than of meeting the demands of the small union recently formed. Air conditioning was impossible, and in the humid summer the few slow fans that hung from the ceiling did little but blow lint. Glenneth had trouble breathing that year. It started slowly, just being a little stuffy in the morning, but it gradually worsened till by the end of the day she felt as if she were gasping. Finally she had gone to Mr. Phillips.

"We need a fan down on my line," she told him. "A big one. There's just no air down there, and we're choking to death."

"No one else's complained," he told her, smiling as if it were just one of those woman things he ignored at times.

"Well, I'm complaining. I can't breathe. I've worked here twenty-some-odd years, and all I'm asking for is a fan."

"I'd have to order it, Glenneth. You know that. By the time it got here, the hot weather'd be over."

"Then give me that one." She pointed to a small fan set on his filing cabinet.

"I thought you wanted a big one."

"I do. But I'll just put that one on my machine, and it'll do me till the other one gets here."

"What about the other women?"

"You just said no one complained but me."

She got the fan, and if the other women made jokes about her and her funny ways, she didn't mind. People always talked about women alone, always read meanings and oddness into normal things. Glenneth tried to treat people fair in spite of who or what they were, and she figured they should do the same with her. The ones who hogged the work paid for it, she figured. The ones who made little remarks about women who didn't need a man paid for it, too, or would. Maybe she wasn't close to any of the women. Maybe she wasn't close to anybody, but where was the rule that said she had to be? Some people were born just not needing anyone.

The big clock hanging on the wall above the machines read ten o'clock—break time. The noise died down as the machines stopped, the newly finished pockets or sleeves sliding into the canvas bags behind each machine. Glenneth hurried to the coffee dispenser and took the lukewarm coffee with her to the office. It was closed by a partition, half-wood, half-glass. Mr. Phillips was waiting behind his desk. He motioned her in.

"How you been, Glenneth?"

"Been fine, like always."

"You ever been sick?"

"Not so anyone'd know. Why?"

"You're getting on." He said it softly, not bantering like usual. Glenneth kept her knees primly together beneath the lavender print dress. She hadn't given in like some of the older girls; she still wore only dresses to work. Just like she always put on a little sachet at break time. "We're all getting on," she said. "You been here as long as I have."

"Doesn't show behind a desk."

Glenneth knew then why she'd been called in. She didn't want to believe it, but she knew. How many years had she managed the piecework? So many she couldn't remember. Always went above the quota. Still did, didn't she? She tried to recall her last check. What had it been? She had deposited it without really looking. It didn't take much to live, the house was paid for, and she just deposited the check as usual.

"You call me in here to tell me I'm getting on?" She tried to keep her voice light. The manager traced something invisible on the desk blotter with his finger.

"Thinking about moving you to something different."

"I like piecework."

"Everybody likes piecework. Everybody wants it."

"I been on that line for years."

"I know, Glenneth. Too long." He looked up at her. "You haven't met the quota, or just barely met it, for weeks now. Three months, really. Line supervisor is squawking."

Line supervisor. Melba Spender. Tall and skinny and

thought the title meant she could snicker about a woman's hair or clothes or eating habits. Melba Spender.

"I can pick it up. She should've let me know. Should've come to me first." Glenneth tried to sip the coffee, cold now. She couldn't taste it. "You telling me it's final?"

"Yes. Monday. You go to packaging."

Glenneth nodded and pushed up from the chair. He was looking at her. He was a kind man. She wouldn't say anything. Not now. She couldn't. She closed the door behind her and walked back to the line. Packaging. She knew what she'd be doing. Going after the canvas bags on wheels that caught the finished work, leaving an empty one. Keeping the quick hands stocked. Walking, trying to see who needed what. She swallowed. She put a new spool on her machine. She had oiled this machine, cared for it better than the factory mechanic did. She never had to call him like some of the girls. In her purse was a small kit of tools, a screwdriver, pliers. When Melba Spender walked by, Glenneth didn't look up.

The pain started about one o'clock, but Frank stayed the rest of the afternoon. The cushion didn't help. Nothing did. But it wouldn't have been any different at home. Worse, maybe, because he couldn't keep it from his face, and then Wilma got frantic. Not in her movements, because there was nothing she could do, but frantic in her eyes and breathing and the shape of her mouth. She was a good woman, Wilma was. Always had been a good wife. But she looked at him now as if she expected something all the time.

In his yard again, Frank laid the fish on the small chopping block he had built in the lower part of the yard. Old Tom had been waiting as if he knew in advance that Frank would bring home fish. He lay now a few feet away, fat, eyes closed, seeming unconcerned.

"Frank. Please come in." Wilma stood on the back steps, her arms over her belly, the blue sweater hugged tight.

"Just a minute." He could have thrown away the fish, and she wouldn't have known.

"Frank."

"Okay. I've just got to clean this up." He heard the door close behind her.

"Saw Tom sitting on your side. Figured you'd been out fishing." Glenneth was standing near her fence, the wind whipping the print dress around her thick legs.

"Don't know how he always knows. You like some fish, Glenneth?"

"Don't like it."

They'd been through this before, but he always offered. "How's work?"

"Okay. About the same." She looked up at the clouds. "We're going to have a big one."

"Yeah. Been brewing all day."

The back door slammed, and Wilma called again, raising her hand a little to wave. Glenneth waved back and turned toward her own home. She sat at her table as usual, the chicken she had fried turning out golden and crisp. She thought thirty-one years should matter. Always a good worker, on time, didn't spread out the break, didn't make extra runs to the women's room. Didn't cause trouble. Only way she could make it to the pension was by making it the next four years, and she didn't know if she could do it. Not in packaging. Pushing, lifting. She laid down the chicken leg. She wasn't even hungry, and she was always hungry. She had never felt old before.

Frank tried to keep it from showing. He ate a little of everything Wilma fixed, but it didn't work. He saw her watching him, saw the set of her mouth, her eyes changing with the worry.

"It's bad, isn't it?" she asked, and he shook his head.

"No. I'm tired. You were right. I should have rested."

"I'm going to call Dr. Massey. Tell him you'll start the treatment again."

"No."

"I'm going to do it. I'm just going to do it, Frank. I can't just sit here and watch . . ." She buried her face in her hands, slender hands, with only a few dark spots on the skin. He wanted to comfort her, but he couldn't. There was nothing he could do. He thought of it again, that nausea deep in the bones, so deep you couldn't throw it up, throw it out. The pain hit him, and he gripped the table, glad Wilma's face was still buried. Sweat ran down his chest, cold; he thought he would pass out, wished he would pass out, but he sat with no sound coming from his lips till the pain gradually ebbed away.

"I'm going fishing tomorrow," he said, and left the room.

Glenneth set the timer in the kitchen for thirty minutes and lay on the sofa with her feet propped up. She had

never needed to rest after work before, not until bedtime, the way it should be. She closed her eyes, seeing
the work cart empty, then full, the way the others looked
at her as she pushed between the lines, bringing work,
taking work. Seeing Melba Spender, only forty. When
the timer buzzed, Glenneth found her house slippers,
walked into the kitchen. She began peeling potatoes for
her dinner. She wouldn't start snacking, like some people did. She'd eat regular meals, at the table. Through
the window she could see Frank in his backyard. He
hadn't given up the fishing yet. She pushed back the curtains with one hand, watching him. Things changed so.
One day he wouldn't be out there. One summer old
Tom would be at her house every day. Wilma would give
up the house maybe; new people would move in. She had
never been close to Frank and Wilma, but they were
good people, good neighbors. Frank had helped Glenneth once when a possum had been caught up in the
attic, helped her get the beehive out of the old china-
berry tree in the front. Some winter mornings he had
helped her get her car started.

Outside, Frank leaned suddenly, over the block, his
head dipping down till the collar of the heavy coat hid his
face. Glenneth dropped the potato and knife into the
sink and hurried to the back door. She stopped, looked
around her, and grabbed the sack of trash from the basket. In the yard she glanced in his direction as she put
the bag in the barrel by the shed. He still hadn't straightened. She walked toward her low fence, seeing him from
the corner of her eye while she called to the cat.

"Tom, you fat old thing, why don't you come home?
It's almost winter."

Frank rose. His eyes were sunken, the pores of his skin enlarged so that the stubble showed more.

"Hi, Glenneth."

She nodded, looked at the sky, back at the cat, but saw that Frank's face was still blanched.

"You're getting him fat."

"It's getting cold. He needs some weight."

"Guess so. Probably snow before Thanksgiving."

"Yeah. One of those years." Frank slowly pushed all the scraps together on the block and stepped away from it, toward the fence and Glenneth.

"How's work going?"

Glenneth wrapped her arms around her waist. "Fine," she said. "Just fine."

"That's good."

They watched Tom jump on the block, his body curving protectively around the scraps.

"He's been a good old Tom, hasn't he, Glenneth?"

"He has. Mean. No ears. Half a tail."

"He's been something, all right."

They watched the cat quietly. Frank pushed his hands in his pockets, smiled a little. The air had turned cooler, the Missouri night wind beginning. Glenneth pulled her arms closer. Frank's eyes were blue. She didn't remember ever knowing what color they were before.

"They put me in packaging," she said.

"Packaging? Is that good?"

"Where they put old people. Don't bother me much, though." She looked away from him, down. "Thought maybe I'd put some bulbs in here this weekend." She bent, pulled leaves away from the small slats of the fence. "Look nice next spring."

"Thought they had a union down at the factory."

"They do. Piece prices, pensions, that sort of thing. Think Wilma'd mind having some tulips along here?

"No. It'd be nice."

On Saturday, Frank's son and his family came. Frank sat in his recliner, watching the game with Dave and the boy. He had never seen his grandson so quiet, just sitting, thin legs awkwardly crossed, finger tapping against the arm of the sofa. Dave didn't tease Wilma about the overheated house. They all talked and laughed a little, but it seemed as if they were in a church or a sickroom. Even the murmur of voices from the kitchen, Wilma and Rosie, seemed different. Frank closed his eyes. When he opened them, he caught Dave staring at him with Wilma's expression. Such dark eyes. The boy had them, too. "I can't do a goddamn thing about it, Dave," he said. "Not a goddamn thing." Then he couldn't talk anymore.

When they left, Frank wouldn't go back in the house with Wilma. He sat on the porch swing, hands in his lap, staring at the road in front of his house and the homes across it. Prairie Street. When he moved here, it hadn't been paved and had no name. When cars went by, dust filtered into the house and settled on the furniture until Wilma spread cheesecloth across the front windows. They had wanted to live in a small town for Dave, in a good neighborhood, with the same friends. A small place where they still caroled at Christmas, had town raffles for turkeys at Thanksgiving. It had been a good little town.

A door slammed shut next door. Glenneth had stepped down from her porch and was crossing her yard with a cardboard box and trowel. He walked to her. She had on her working clothes: an old dress covered with a gray sweater, black and white oxfords with gray socks, men's leather gloves and a scarf. She had dressed the same, year in and out, when she worked in the yard in the fall. In the spring it would be only slightly different: no sweater and a hat in place of the scarf. She had knelt and was clearing the soil for the bulbs. He watched her for awhile, then walked around to his backyard and took his tools from the rack in the shed.

He talked to her about the bulbs; about the broken slats, if it had been his grandson who broke them; about the lopsided tree, if it should come out or maybe would stand up under the next high wind; about whether the town was really going to build a housing project on the slope above and beyond the ditch. Glenneth answered him as she always had, practically, wanting to keep the tree whatever happened, not trusting the town to do what was right: if they built the project the foundations would wash down the slope with the rain. But her voice seemed strained, and she rested often, sitting back on her heels and looking down the fence line at the soil still to be broken.

"How's work going?"

"Fine," she said. "Just fine."

Frank pushed a bulb deep and smoothed the dirt above it. "They still got you in packaging?"

She nodded and moved away, pushing the box of bulbs before her.

"You ought to talk to that union."

"Can't."

"That's what it's for."

She didn't answer. She shook her head and a few moments later shook it again.

When Frank woke in the night now Wilma fixed him hot milk as his mother had done in his childhood illnesses. Wilma bought the candy he liked and kept it in every room of the house. "Eat, Frank, please," she said. On the kitchen counter was a schedule. Wilma timed the medication, the dosage. He tried not to ask for it, and every time he did, it was too soon. Wilma slept in a cot next to his bed at night so he could sleep easier, and he couldn't make her not do this. She had lost weight, wouldn't go shopping on Mondays as she always had but instead let Rosie do the grocery buying, the small errands. He called Dr. Massey and asked for something to help Wilma relax, but she wouldn't take the pills.

The weather was cold, the wind strong. Wilma closed the drapes against the chill, but he made her open them. It seemed to him there was a quickness outside, the cars speeding, the kids running, laughing, the wind blowing. Even the first snow seemed to fall in a hurry, heavy and wet. Only Glenneth moved slowly. He saw how she sat in her car now when she came home from work and how she placed her hand on the porch post before stepping up. On the morning after the snow, her car wouldn't start, and he tried to take his peacoat from the closet, but Wilma stopped him. "She can call the garage, Frank. You can't do this." He watched the mechanic come, put the jumper cables on. Such a simple thing.

The weather warmed again right before Christmas. Frank used the cane to walk in the backyard. The chopping block had darkened, only a few half-rotted leaves lying on its surface. He brushed them off, leaned against the wood. This summer the Castor would flow on, the trees bush out, wild honeysuckle line the roadway. But there would be no fish. Not for Frank Cauley. Maybe Tom would sit under the tree and wait. Maybe for the whole summer. Maybe Glenneth would come get him, take him into her yard. He looked toward her house. The dish was by the back steps. "Tom?" he called. "Hey. Tom." He stepped over the fence and crossed the yard. The dish was empty, a thick ring where the milk had set awhile before Tom had come. But no cat. He stood looking at the back door where white curtains with pink flowers were stretched tight over the glass pane. He knocked.

"Frank. Well, I never. You just come in."

"Looking for Tom."

"You come on in here. Sit down. I've got to get some shoes on. Just put these slippers on for a minute and forgot to change."

Her kitchen smelled like food, a roast, maybe, in the oven. There were plants on the windowsills, except above the sink. His daughter-in-law kept plants like that, in every room of the house.

"How's Wilma?" she called from the bedroom.

"Fine."

"Haven't seen you out lately." He heard her pause. "But it's been cold."

"It has. Been a bad one this year."

Glenneth took cups from the cupboard, poured coffee. She wouldn't sit down till she had put out sugar and cream, although he wanted neither, and had placed napkins on the table.

"That Tom was here this morning," she said. "Just like always."

"Thought I'd look at him. See how he was doing."

Frank sipped the coffee. The windows of her kitchen were steamy. The wallpaper she had added was yellow, the seams not matching close to the ceiling. She had done it herself, just like she mowed her own yard, pruned her own trees.

"How's work?"

"Fine. Just fine."

"Glenneth, that union. You paid for it."

Her hand smoothed against the table. It was a thick hand, looked stronger than Wilma's.

"They say I can't do the work anymore. The union can't do a thing about that."

"They owe it to you."

"Don't anybody owe anybody anything." She stood, took his cup to the stove and filled it. When she set it in front of him again, it rattled a little against the saucer. "You won't have them treatments," she said.

"No."

She sat back down, her hand brushing against the table again. "It scares me to go to the union."

"Those treatments make me sick." Frank shook his head. "So damned sick."

The winter was a long one, and hard, rain turning to sleet, then freezing solid. It was early April before a warm day came and the same month that Frank's treatments stopped the final time. Glenneth didn't visit. It had never been her way to visit. She worked at her machine and tried to make the quota; it seemed to her that the work had become harder.

She had expected to hear from Wilma when it happened, but it was Frank's son who told her, standing on her porch and speaking to her through the screen. When he left, she walked through her house and stepped outside. She would put in a garden again this year, maybe paint the front porch. She pulled her arms tightly against her. Down the yard the old lopsided tree had made it through another winter; the slope beyond had been cleared by the city. She walked toward her fence. The flowers had pushed up, still small, fragile. Old Tom lay among them, the sun shining against his gray fur, making him look sleek and young. "Tom," she said, and he raised his head. She picked him up and carried him toward her back door. "Tom, it's summer."

Text design by Jillian Downey
Typesetting by Delmastype, Ann Arbor, Michigan
Font: Mrs Eaves

Zuzana Licko designed the font Mrs Eaves in
1996, for the digital type foundry Emigre.
　　　　　　　　　—courtesy www.myfonts.com